A Trick of the Light
The Pages of Time Book 1.5

Damian Knight

The story so far...

After suffering a traumatic brain injury in the crash of Flight 0368, a shocking terrorist attack that killed his father and left his mother in a coma, sixteen-year-old Sam Rayner wakes in hospital to discover he has developed seizures during which he is transported into the body of his past or future self.

Sam collapses at his father's funeral and suddenly finds himself flung several hours ahead, where he learns about a bomb blast at Thames House, the headquarters of the British Security Service. Upon returning to the present, he tips off the police, thereby preventing the atrocity and inadvertently drawing the attention of Lara McHayden, head of the Tempus Project, a secret government organisation investigating people with alleged time-travelling capabilities.

McHayden offers Sam the chance to control his ability and help track down rogue MI5 agent Esteban Haufner, the man responsible for both the foiled Thames House bombing and the sabotage of Flight 0368. Using Tetradyamide – a drug originally developed during the Vietnam War by McHayden's long-lost fiancé, Isaac Barclay – Sam begins training at the Tempus Research Facility, a subterranean complex outside of London.

He is not, however, the only person to have developed such abilities; almost half a century earlier, Michael Humboldt, a soldier who sustained a similar injury during the Vietnam War, escaped a secure military hospital in California under mysterious circumstances. McHayden believes that Humboldt is responsible for turning Haufner, and asks Sam to help capture him. In doing so, Sam becomes caught in a web of lies and manipulation that threaten to destroy everyone and everything he holds dear.

Now, in *A Trick of the Light*, we journey back to 1960s California to witness the events that will lead Michael Humboldt to become a wanted man, and unearth the true circumstances behind Isaac Barclay's unsolved disappearance.

CONTENTS

Chapter I

The Bird that Flew its Cage

1

July 1969

On the first occasion Michael tried to pick the lock of his cell, the pin of Dr McHayden's brooch snapped, cutting his palm. With Dr Barclay's miracle drug sending a euphoric shiver through his body, the sensation of pain was strangely muted. He stepped back and glanced down at the blood oozing over silver and pearl. A scarlet droplet seeped between his fingers and splashed onto the leg of the oversize pants he'd appropriated for his escape. Smiling, he closed his left eye, the one that wasn't covered by a cloth patch. From the darkness pinpricks of colour emerged, spinning and spiralling in a merry dance. They grew and grew, coming together to form the picture of a broken, bloodstained brooch in his hand.

'Back,' he said, and the picture obeyed. The stain withdrew from his leg, coalescing into a droplet of blood that, when complete, rose up like a balloon before slipping in between his fingers. He saw himself step to the door again. The blood on his hand drained into the cut, which then melted closed.

And just like that, the brooch was whole once more.

Michael blinked and was surrounded by the real world, the one filled with movements, sounds and smells. Turning the brooch over in his hand, he inspected the seamless hinge that, just a moment before, had been broken in two.

'Beautiful. A truly beautiful thing,' he said aloud, and then sniggered, for there was no one to hear him speak.

Going slowly so as to not repeat his mistake, he inserted the pin in the lock again. Before the explosion that had brought him to Stribe Lyndhurst Military Hospital earlier that year, he had been right-handed, and his left hand still felt clumsy and poorly coordinated by comparison. Applying gentle pressure, he jiggled and twisted, probed and coerced, until eventually the tumblers clunked open.

Peering out through the door, he found the corridor of the secure unit deserted. As he stepped from his cell, a memory hit him like a blow to the head: when six years old, Michael had been struck down with tonsillitis. He remembered his mother leaning over, humming a tune and mopping his brow with a damp cloth while he lay shivering in bed. At one point she had swept back her hair to reveal a brooch pinned to the breast of her dress. Silver and pearl, it was, and it had gleamed in the dim illumination of his bedside lamp.

The recollection stopped Michael midstride. Opening his fist, he gazed down upon the brooch swiped from Dr McHayden's blouse a short while earlier. It was so alike the one his mother had worn all those years ago as to be almost identical, but however much he longed to keep it, it didn't belong to him, and his mother (rest her soul) had by no means raised a common thief.

Suppressing a stab of regret, he returned briefly to his cell and placed the brooch in the middle of the neatly made bed, then limped back into the corridor and over to the gate at the far end. As he'd been counting on, it had been left unlocked again and hung ajar.

Here he paused to catch his breath and massage the stump of his right arm, where his new prosthetic – an ugly, cumbersome thing with a metal hook for a hand – still rubbed and chafed.

After intercepting the attack on his base in Vietnam at the cost of an eye, a forearm and a traumatic brain injury, Michael had ended up incarcerated, treated like some kind of freak or wrongdoer instead of the hero he was. But since Dr Barclay had begun using him as a human guinea pig in his unauthorised drug trials, a plan had taken shape. Once Michael realised he could not pass back to the time before his injuries and therefore undo them, the ensuing weeks had been spent in preparation for this moment: the day the bird would finally fly its cage.

So far everything was going to plan. He had rehearsed this stage of his escape on numerous occasions, although what lay ahead was far less certain and needed to be timed to perfection. But then again, the beauty of Dr Barclay's drug was that timing could be tweaked and honed almost indefinitely.

After a minute or two's rest, he stepped through the gate, closed it behind him and began down the second corridor of the Lincoln Ward. It seemed strangely quiet, the assorted moans and groans that accompanied day and night in the secure unit conspicuously absent. Three quarters down, he came across a man in a wheelchair whose entire head was wrapped with white bandage.

'Hi, how are you?' Michael asked, drawing his shoulders back as he approached.

The dark eyes behind a narrow slit in the bandage followed him every step of the way, but the man neither spoke nor otherwise moved.

Michael opened the swing doors to the third and final corridor of the Lincoln Ward. Watercolour landscapes hung intermittently on the walls, suggesting happier climes. The rooms off this corridor had no locks on the doors, leaving patients free to come and go as they pleased, and a small group of men were sat around a foldout table at the far end, shooting the breeze over a game of cards.

He attempted striding purposefully by as though he had more important matters on his mind, but as he drew level, one of the men – a short fellow with a fleshy hook for a nose – called out, 'Holy Moses! What the heck happened to you?'

Michael flinched at the barb, but tried to ignore it and continue on his way, when all of a sudden Hooknose jumped out of his seat and caught him by the arm.

'Sorry, pal, didn't mean no offense by it. Speak first, think later. Or that's what my wife says.' He released Michael's arm and held out his hand. 'The name's Edgar Mitchell, but call me Mitch. Everyone else does.'

'I'm Michael.'

'Pleased to make your acquaintance, Michael. You new here? Only I don't recall seeing you about before.'

'Something like that.'

'Well welcome to the Lincoln Ward. You want to join me and the fellas for a hand of poker? We're only playing for smokes.'

The offer of company was such a rare treat that Michael actually found himself considering it. Then he realised he was wasting valuable seconds. 'Another time,' he said and made to turn away.

At that moment a chorus of cheers erupted from the direction of the front desk, followed by the sound of a champagne cork popping. He paced to the end of the corridor, drew himself close to the wall and poked his head around the corner. A large crowd of hospital staff had gathered by the entrance to the Lincoln Ward, and were back-slapping and toasting one another with paper cups.

Michael was too late: Apollo 11 was already down and the moment was lost.

As he watched on, a couple – a man and a woman – broke away from the main group and began strolling toward him. Pulling his head back, he squeezed his body tight to the wall. It was that mean, po-faced nurse with bleached-blonde hair – Mclean, her name was – and the ward janitor, Hank Windle.

As the clip-clopping of Mclean's shoes drew closer, Michael heard her giggle and say, 'This way, Hank. I know someplace we won't be disturbed.'

He turned and hurried back toward the card-playing soldiers. Mitch, the man who'd invited him to join them, was standing in the same spot, watching him with a puzzled expression.

'You know, maybe I will join you for a game after all,' Michael said.

Mitch continued to stare. 'Say, you sure you should be here?'

Before Michael could answer, there was a loud gasp a few feet away. He glanced back to see Hank Windle lunge at him, arms outstretched. The janitor tackled him around the waist, and together they tumbled into the fold-out table, sending a plume of playing cards cascading into the air. Michael thrashed to free himself, but Windle rose first and straddled him across the chest, while Mitch grabbed him around the legs.

'Keep him there, I'll fetch Dr Barclay!' Mclean yelled, and darted off toward the front desk.

As Michael lay on the floor, his chest crushed under Windle's weight, a card – the seven of clubs – drifted down and settled on his forehead. Smiling, he closed his eye again. From the darkness, dots of coloured light sprang forth, like shooting stars in a night sky. They expanded, merging together to form the picture of Windle sitting astride him, teeth gritted under a bushy moustache.

'Back,' he commanded.

With a shudder, the picture began to reverse. The seven of clubs floated up and away from his forehead. Windle clambered off his chest and dragged him upright. Grappling, they backed into the upturned table, which righted itself on impact. Dispersed playing cards rose through the air, briefly forming a nebulous cloud around them before dropping into neat piles on the table's surface. Suddenly Windle released him and sprang back, landing a few feet away with his arms outstretched.

Michael's view shifted as his body rotated to face Mitch, who was staring at him with that puzzled expression again. Then, facing the wrong way, he backtracked to the end of the corridor, where he squeezed up against the wall and poked his head around the corner just in time to see Windle and Mclean back away, separate and merge with the crowd around the front desk.

At that point things started to speed up. He jerked his head back and retreated down the corridor. Reaching the card game, he stopped for a brief, silent exchange with Mitch before passing through the swing doors. The strange, bandaged man watched him every step of the way as he backed down the second corridor of the Lincoln Ward. As he approached the secure unit, the gate swung open, allowing him to pass through unimpeded. On the other side, he saw himself pause to lean against the wall, his chest falling and rising with each breath.

It was only as Michael straightened up and limped back to his cell that he mouthed the word, 'Stop.'

The flickering, backward-playing pictures ground to a halt. He blinked and the world around him gained motion, a temporal U-turn that made his stomach flip.

This time, instead of pausing to catch his breath, he staggered straight through the gate and down the second corridor, beads of sweat trickling down the sides of his face.

The man in the wheelchair watched him approach.

'Don't suppose you feel like an field trip?' Michael asked.

Once again the man said nothing.

'I'll take that as a yes,' Michael said, unclipping the brakes of the chair. 'Y'know, I could do with a change of scenery myself.' Grasping the left handle with his hand and resting the metal hook of his prosthetic on the right one, he swung the wheelchair around and pushed it through the swing doors to the third corridor.

Mitch and his friends barely glanced up on this occasion. Michael wheeled his new companion right past them and, without slowing his pace, rounded the corner at the end of the corridor. The crowd were now standing in rapt silence, their backs turned and their collective attention held by a television set positioned on a foldout table in the doorway to the office behind the front desk. He gave them a wide berth, but not single person looked up as he pushed the wheelchair out of the Lincoln Ward and into the hall beyond.

At the elevator he stopped, hit the button and applied the brakes on the wheelchair. As the doors opened a chorus of cheers erupted from the front desk, followed by the sound of a champagne cork popping.

'It's been a blast,' Michael said, turning to the bandaged man, 'but, for you at least, our little excursion ends here.'

2

In this new reality Michael didn't witness Neil Armstrong become the first person to set foot on the moon; at that very moment he was using the distraction to sneak onto a near-empty train destined for Denver after an afternoon spent sponging sympathy drinks in a bar near Union Square. Once on board, he managed to maintain the upper hand in a game of hide and seek with the conductor for the best part of an hour until he was finally apprehended in the bathroom and turfed out at Davis, the stop before Sacramento.

With the dipping sun in his face, he trudged north along Route 113. The pain of walking grew unbearable after an hour or two. Davis was behind him, and as dusk settled a blanket of undiluted starlight filled the sky. By now Dr Barclay's miracle drug was wearing off, leaving a deflated emptiness in its wake, but with no other clear plan of action he kept going, plodding along in darkness intermittently broken by passing headlights.

After another mile he came across a remote farm. The lights in the main building were on, but Michael slipped through the unlocked door of the barn, where he gulped down stagnant water from a trough before flopping exhausted onto a bed of hay behind a tractor.

The next morning Michael woke to the sound of a cockerel calling in his second day of freedom. He sat up, brushing pieces of straw from his clothes. The barn was lit by narrow bars of sunlight creeping in between the gaps in the slats. He clambered to his feet, went to the door and peered out. The farmyard was bathed in a dawn glow and apparently devoid of human activity. Not wanting to risk discovery, he drank quickly from the trough again, splashed water over his face and then made his way back to road and continued north.

As dawn gave way to full daylight and the temperature steadily climbed, progress slowed to a snail's pace. The blisters on his feet that had risen overnight now split, filling his shoes with blood and puss. Sunburn ruptured the recently healed skin of his face, and his stump was rubbed raw against the socket of his prosthetic arm.

It was difficult to gauge how long he staggered along the side of the road like that, his stomach rumbling and the occasional passing car spraying him with dust, but eventually he stumbled to his knees, unable to go on any farther.

The game was up, his grand plan of escape in tatters. Choking back tears, he dragged himself to a rock a few yards from the road and sat there, gently sobbing while he waited for the police to pick him up.

It could have been a minute, it could have been an hour, but at some point he was startled by the nearby blare of a horn. Looking up, he saw a beat-up VW camper van waiting on the scorched dirt by the side of the road. A woman with long, dark hair held back in a leather thong was leaning out of the window.

'Hey, cat,' she called, her voice sultry and melodic, 'you lookin' for a ride?'

Michael blinked. Was this a trick of his water-deprived mind? Or perhaps a glimpse of some future event waiting farther down the line? Either way, it was a welcome solution to his current predicament, so he nodded, picked himself up, dusted his hand on the seat of his pants and approached the van.

'Cool.' The woman reached over her shoulder and slid the rear door open. 'Jump in.'

Michael clambered onto the back seat and settled among a pile of embroidered cushions. There was a man behind the wheel. He had hair almost as long as the woman's and was wearing glasses with round, blue-tinted lenses.

'I'm Eagle,' he said, swinging the camper van back onto the road. 'And this here's Toni.'

'*Eagle*?' Michael repeated. 'Like the bird?'

'Exactly. Like the bird.'

'Sure, okay then. I'm Michael.'

'Good to meet you. So, Michael, when'd you get back from Nam?'

'What gave it away?'

Eagle gave a half-hearted laugh and pulled his hair back on one side. The skin around his neck and jaw was bubbled and burned, with a fleshy crater all that remained of his ear. 'Napalm,' he explained, letting his hair fall back. 'I think I'm what's known as collateral damage.'

'Hand grenade,' Michael said, and lifted the patch covering his missing eye.

'What is it about boys and comparing scars?' Toni asked, caressing the passing air through the open window by her side.

Eagle cracked a smile and looked at Michael in the rear view mirror. 'Never mind, man. What's done is done. Anyway, you know what they say, what doesn't kill you makes you stranger.'

'Don't you mean *stronger*?'

'You feel any stronger?'

Michael hesitated, remembering the surge of invincibility he'd felt under the influence of Dr Barclay's drug. 'I guess that depends on what I'm taking.'

Eagle laughed. 'Ain't that the truth! So, Toni and me are headed north. What about you?'

Michael turned to watch the roadside speed by outside. 'North works for me,' he said, and leaned back in his seat.

Michael woke with a start. Rubbing sleep from his eye, he sat up and peered through the dusty window of the stationary camper van. The sun had sunk behind a distant line of redwoods, painting the sky above in delicate shades of pink and orange. Toni had moved to the driver's seat, but Eagle was nowhere about.

'Where are we?' Michael asked.

'Stopped for gas.' She turned to face him. 'You need the restroom or something?'

Although he wasn't sure how long he'd been asleep, the pressure in his bladder, crick in his neck and pins and needles in his legs suggested it was at least several hours. 'That might be an idea,' he said, and slid the rear door open. 'You won't leave without me, right?'

'Wouldn't dream of it, cat.'

The evening was already several degrees cooler than the night before, causing Michael to shiver as he crossed the asphalt of a two-pump gas station. The restrooms were out of order, but there was a note on the door directing customers to use the facilities at the Redwood Diner instead.

Letting out a sigh, he turned back and crossed the road to the rundown diner on the other side. It was only then that he noticed the muddy, bullet-ridden sign by the roadside:

STAPLETON, HUMBOLDT COUNTY
WE WELCOME CARFEUL DRIVERS!

He stopped and stared. When Michael was a kid, his mother had told him that his paternal grandfather, Gerhardt von Humboldt, was a German immigrant who'd dropped the 'von' part of the name around the outbreak of World War II. Michael had tried raising the subject with Pa a few years later, but his father had quickly grown angry and shouted him down, as he always did when confronted by something that made him uncomfortable. In all the years since, Michael had never so much as heard the name in passing, and when Pa had died a few weeks ago he had assumed that he was the last Humboldt left. And yet here was a whole *county* that bore his family name. If such a discovery wasn't an omen then he wasn't sure what was.

'Ready?' Eagle said, suddenly appearing by Michael's side with a bag of potato chips in one hand and a six-pack of beer in the other. 'We can be in Eureka in under an hour if we burn rubber.'

At that moment the door of the diner opened, allowing a segment of snatched conversation to escape. A waitress stepped out, heaving a refuse sack that clanked with empty bottles. She was young, probably close to Michael's age, had long, auburn hair tied back in a yellow ribbon and was without doubt the most beautiful girl he'd ever seen.

Mesmerised, he watched as she hauled the sack to a dumpster and deposited it inside. As she turned back, she glanced up and caught Michael staring, but instead of flinching or looking away like almost everyone else did when first confronted by his appearance, she smiled warmly.

'Michael?' Eagle said, nudging him in the bicep. 'You coming?'

'Huh?'

'We better hit the road. You coming with or what?'

Michael looked back to see the waitress disappear through the door to the diner again. Taped to the inside of the window was a sign: HELP WANTED.

'No,' he said. 'I think I might stick around a while.'

Chapter II

Meaningful Employment

1

December 1969

Michael moved to one side as Ellis Conway, the proprietor of the Redwood Diner, stepped to the hotplate with a spatula in hand. With a deft flick of his wrist, Ellis flipped three sizzling patties over, then cracked an egg on top of each. This demonstration of the proper construction of the diner's trademark Redwood Burger was not what held Michael's attention, however: his focus was firmly on Rachel, Ellis's eighteen-year-old daughter, as she circled the tables of the restaurant like a ballerina.

Rachel Conway was the waitress Michael had seen the day after fleeing San Francisco. On that fateful summer's evening, he had followed her into the diner. Seeking any excuse to speak to her, he had asked about the HELP WANTED sign in the window. It was a decision that would alter the course of his life, for Rachel had introduced Michael to her father, who'd invited him back the next day for his first shift as a kitchen hand.

In the five months since, things were starting to look up. When Michael had arrived in Humboldt County it was with nothing – even the shirt on his back was pilfered from Hank Windle's janitor's closet – but now, under the alias 'Harrison' and the fictional backstory of a childhood house fire that had caused his injuries and left him orphaned, he had employment, a room in a boarding house where his savings (over fifty bucks already) were stashed in a tin under a loose floorboard and, most significantly, a newfound purpose in life, for ever since that first glimpse of Rachel, his sole aim had been to win her heart.

'Could use some more buns over here,' Ellis said, not looking up from the hotplate.

Michael averted his adoring gaze from Rachel. 'Huh?'

'Buns, Michael. Need some more, if you think you can fit it into your schedule.'

'Oh right, sure.'

Michael crossed the kitchen and let himself into the storeroom. As he reached for the box of burger buns on the top of the shelving unit at the back, he caught a glimpse of his reflection in the side of a pan on the shelf below. The appearance of his scars had markedly improved since the summer, and a couple of weeks ago he had invested in a new eye patch – leather instead of the frayed cotton strip he'd been issued in hospital – but was there really any chance a girl like Rachel could look beyond his physical defects and return his feelings for her, or had he somehow confused pity for affection?

His throat tightened and his good mood dissipated. Suddenly he became aware of the sound of drumming blood behind his ears, which was more often than not a precursor to one of his seizures. Thankfully, the fits that had plagued him during his miserable imprisonment at

Stribe Lyndhurst had faded to more of a background whisper, and of the handful of incidents in recent months, all had occurred in the solitude of his room, where doubt so often crept into his mind during the dark and lonely nights.

He gulped, pulled a fresh pack of buns from the box and turned away from his reflection. Back in high school, he had been relentlessly bullied about his weight and, as a consequence, always felt awkward around girls. But that had never been the case with Rachel; they had so much in common that conversation flowed as naturally as water down a hill. She had also lost her mother at an early age and had been raised by her father, although by all accounts Ellis had made a much better stab at the task than Pa. Like Michael, Rachel felt herself an outsider in the backwater town of her birth, and longed to escape and fulfil her ambitions of travelling the world as a dancer. They spoke of these things and many more during the long, tedious spells when the diner was customerless and there was little else to occupy the time. He had bared his soul to her, revealing desires and insecurities that he had never shared with anyone else. And one day soon – maybe even today, if he got the chance – Michael would pluck up the courage to tell Rachel how he truly felt.

With a sigh, he returned to the kitchen and handed the buns to Ellis, who fished three out, laid each on a separate plate next to a serving of fries and then slid the egg-covered patties on top, followed by a slice of avocado and a wedge of blue cheese. When the orders were good to go, Ellis lined them up along the heated counter between the kitchen and the restaurant, then hit the button on a silver bell.

'I need to go out for a bit,' he said, offering Michael the spatula. 'You mind holding the fort? I'll be twenty minutes, tops.'

'Are you sure, Ellis?'

'Come on, you must've seen me flip a thousand burgers by now. I think you got this, Michael.'

Rachel arrived to collect the orders. A strand of auburn hair had escaped her ribbon – blue today – and hung down across her finely freckled cheekbone. She brushed it away, smiled at Michael, transferred the plates to a tray and then whisked them away.

'Okay, I'll do it,' Michael said.

Ellis handed him the spatula, lifted his apron over his head and exchanged it for a sheepskin coat hanging on the back of the door. 'If anyone orders something you can't manage, just stall them and I'll take care of it when I get back. But it's pretty quiet in here, I'd be surprised if you have to lift a finger.'

'I appreciate your trust in me.'

'Don't mention it,' Ellis said, and rested a hand on Michael's shoulder. 'You're a good worker, Michael, and I've enjoyed having you about the place these last few months. I was talking with Rachel the other day. What with you being on your own and all, we were wondering if you'd like to join us for Christmas dinner next week? If you don't already have plans, that is.'

'Plans? No, I'd like that.'

'Good. It won't be anything fancy, just the three of us, but my cranberry sauce is famous throughout the county.' He gave Michael's shoulder a final squeeze and left through the rear door.

Alone in the kitchen, Michael stepped to the hotplate and surveyed his temporary domain. Mr Sykes, the old-timer who owned the gas station across the road, was at a table in the near corner and had already managed to make a single piece of pie and coffee last over an hour. A young couple with a child – not locals, just passing through – were at a booth at the far side of the restaurant, tucking into the burgers Rachel had just delivered.

In conclusion, then, Ellis had probably been right and Michael wouldn't have to lift a finger, which was a shame, really, since it represented a missed opportunity to prove himself. Looking for something to do, he ambled over to the sink and washed the last few pots and pans – not an easy thing with only one hand, but there was a knack – then set about chipping away the blackened meat welded to the hotplate. At least he now had an alternative to passing the Christmas holidays alone in his room.

After a while the family finished up, paid and left. Rachel cleared the table and pumped a quarter into the jukebox. There was a brief pause and then *Devil in Disguise* blasted out far higher than the volume Ellis normally allowed. Doing a remarkably accurate Elvis leg-shake-hip-wiggle, she strutted over to the hatch to the kitchen and took a stool across the counter.

'You think he'll mind?' Michael asked, dipping his head toward their last remaining customer.

'What, about my dancing?'

'No, dummy, the music. It's kind of loud.'

'Old Man Sykes?' Rachel laughed and span full circle on the rotating seat of her stool. 'The guy served in the artillery corps during World War II. He's so out of it the whole diner could burn down and he'd still be here in the morning, sitting at the same table, probably nursing that same mug of coffee.'

Michael let out an involuntary shudder. One of the most convincing aspects of his backstory was that, after what had happened in Vietnam, he didn't need to fabricate his fear of fire.

'Oh, dang it!' Rachel laid a delicate, long-fingered hand onto his arm. 'That's insensitive of me. I am sorry, I wasn't thinking.'

'It's fine,' he said, the muscles of his arm unclenching at her touch. 'I know it's almost ten years, but there's still not a day goes by I don't think about that night. Probably not even an hour.' He glanced down at the hook of his prosthetic. 'It's kind of hard when you're living with a constant reminder.'

'Shh, let me make it up to you...' She leaned forward and, for a moment, he thought she might kiss him, but then she reached around, opened the hatch on the glass display case and took out a plate holding the final two pieces of apple pie. 'Here, get some spoons and help me out.'

Although Michael got his meals for free, it didn't feel right eating stock, and he knew the business was struggling on account of the new highway that bypassed the town. He opened his mouth to protest, but Rachel rolled her eyes at him.

'Michael, don't be such a square! It'll only go to waste when we close up, and it's almost ten already. You don't honestly believe anyone else is coming in tonight, do you?'

'No, I guess not.'

'Well then, get some spoons like I said. And some ice cream while you're at it.'

He obliged – as if it were ever going any other way – and in less than a minute the plate was empty.

'So,' he said, scraping up the last few crumbs, 'Ellis mentioned me coming over for Christmas Day. I was thinking we could—'

The bell above the door chimed and Jimmy Peltzer walked in. Like most men in the area, Jimmy worked at the sawmill down by the river. He was unmarried, in his late-twenties and lived alone in a shack about a mile out of town. He ate at the diner most evenings but was later than usual today.

After casting a disapproving glance around the diner, he sniffed, wiped his nose on the sleeve of his hunting jacket and took his usual booth by the window.

'Looks like I was wrong then,' Rachel said, and slid off her stool. 'It'll be a burger and fries as usual, but I should probably go check anyway. You know, just in case he's feeling spontaneous.'

'Okay,' Michael said. On several occasions he'd noticed the way Jimmy looked at Rachel when he thought no one was watching, and he hadn't liked it one bit. He went to fetch another patty from the refrigerator, slapped it on the hotplate and then eavesdropped as Rachel took Jimmy's order.

'...I don't know,' he heard her say over the sizzle of cooking meat. 'He should be back any minute.'

'And he left you here, minding store all on your lonesome?'

'I'm not on my "lonesome", Jimmy. Michael's here too.'

'The freak? Jesus, it hurts just looking at the guy.'

'That's mean! Now listen, are you going to order something, or did you just stop by to insult the staff?'

'All right, all right.' Jimmy lifted the menu and studied it with exaggerated consideration. 'I don't know,' he said eventually. 'What do you recommend?'

She placed a hand on her hip. 'Oh man, come on! The menu hasn't changed in all the years you've been coming here.'

'Humour me.'

'The Redwood Burger is especially popular. It's what you have every time.'

He laid the menu flat on the table and smiled. One of his front teeth was chipped and half the size of its partner. 'That sounds just fine, sweetness. Get me fries and a chocolate shake with that, too.'

Rachel snatched the menu from the table. As she turned and made her way back to the kitchen, Michael could see Jimmy's eyes popping out of his head as he ogled her legs.

'The usual,' she said, leaning against the counter.

'It's already on,' Michael told her. 'You shouldn't let him talk to you like that, you know.'

'Who, Jimmy?' She laughed and shook her head. 'He's harmless. I've known him since I was, like, twelve years old.'

'It's the way he looks at you. I know it's none of my business, but it creeps me out.'

She smiled, reached over and rested her hand on his arm again. 'You are sweet, Michael,' she said, looking up at him with emerald-green eyes. 'You'll make some girl very happy one of these days.'

He felt a delightful shiver race through his body. More than anything he wanted to tell her that she was that girl and today was that day, but instead he only blushed and looked away, wondering why Jimmy had to walk in when he did.

'Your burger's on fire.'

Michael glanced down to see smoke rising from the hotplate. Cursing, he flapped a dishcloth, dispersing it, then flipped the patty over. The edges were all charred and black, so he scooped it into the trash, collected a new one from the refrigerator and started over. So far he'd only had a single thing to do, and he wasn't exactly justifying Ellis's trust.

While the second burger cooked, he got to work on Jimmy's shake, then slid the patty onto a bun, placed a slice of avocado and a chunk of cheese on top like Ellis had shown him and, fighting the urge to add a special condiment of his own, poured a mound of fries beside it.

As he hit the bell, Mr Sykes drained the last of his coffee, dropped a crumpled bill on the table and lurched his way to the door with a mumbled farewell.

Michael set about wiping down the mess he'd made, when suddenly a scream reverberated through the diner. He spun around, a damp rag in his hand.

Jimmy was on his feet, gripping Rachel by the wrist while she pulled against him. 'Come on,' he hissed, 'just a kiss, just one little kiss.'

She planted a meaty slap on the side of his face.

Without thinking, Michael burst through the swing door and out into the restaurant. 'Let her go! *Now!*'

Jimmy turned to face him, a red handprint radiating beneath the bristles on his cheek. 'Ah, the freak!' he announced, sneering. 'Get back in the kitchen, freak. This don't concern you.'

Michael took a step closer. There was a throbbing, swishing sound behind his ears: the pump and flow of blood. Doing his best to ignore it, he took another step. 'Ellis left me in charge tonight,' he said, 'so anything that happens under this roof definitely *does* concern me. Why don't you let her go, Jimmy? Go home and sleep it off.'

'You planning on using that?' Jimmy asked, nodding toward Michael's hand.

Michael looked down. Without his realising it, he had picked up one of the kitchen knives on his way out. There were still chunks of onion sticking to the blade. He tightened his grip around the handle and looked back up.

'Don't test me, Jimmy. I said to let her go.'

Jimmy grinned and edged back the corner of his jacket to reveal the pearl handle of a revolver tucked into his waistband.

The thrashing of blood behind Michael's ears had become almost deafening. He visualised lunging at Jimmy with the knife, playing the scene over and over as he gauged the split-second's difference between Jimmy drawing the gun and him getting there first.

After a moment he decided it was too close to call. Taking a step to one side, he placed the knife on the nearest table. 'Okay, Jimmy. What do you say we take this outside and settle it like men?'

Jimmy stared at him, then tilted his head back and gave a deep, full-bellied laugh. 'I'm gonna enjoy this, freak,' he said, and released Rachel so abruptly she crumpled to the floor.

Michael took a deep breath and followed Jimmy to the door. With each step the walls of the diner seemed to pulse as though waves of energy were passing through the building.

'Michael, no,' Rachel pleaded, her face white as she struggled with the tangled folds of her waitress uniform.

Even with both hands, Michael never won a fight in his life, but compared to the prospect of her thinking him a coward, the beating he was about to get didn't seem like much to worry about. 'It's fine,' he said as he passed her. 'I know what I'm doing.'

He followed Jimmy out into a chill evening, and over to a rust-coloured pickup positioned across two bays on the far side of the lot. An easterly wind was kicking up off the ocean and a light rain pattered against the ground. Jimmy removed his jacket, folded it on the hood of his truck, placed his gun on top and started rolling up his shirtsleeves.

There were only a couple of yards between them. Hoping to catch Jimmy off-guard, Michael swung first, but his target dodged all too easily, leaving his fist slicing through thin air.

Jimmy grinned, displaying a mouth full of cracked, uneven teeth. 'You're dead meat now, freak,' he said, winding up.

Michael closed his eye and waited for the blow to land.

It never did.

2

Michael blinked and opened his eye. Jimmy and the parking lot of the Redwood Diner were gone. In their place was the interior of a lavishly decorated hotel suite. A thick cream carpet covered the floor. The walls were lined with embroidered wallpaper. His detached prosthetic arm was lying beside a leather briefcase in the middle of a wide, sumptuous bed several times the size of any he'd seen before, let alone slept on. At the far end of the room a pair of double doors opened onto a balcony, beyond which a city skyline lit up the night: San Francisco.

'What the...?' he muttered, and took an unsteady step forward. His head felt woozy, kind of like he'd been drinking. Glancing down, he saw his bare legs poking out from under a fluffy white bathrobe. The words *The Fairmont Hotel* were stitched to the breast in curling lettering.

It didn't make sense. What was Michael doing back in San Francisco after all the trouble he'd gone to escaping the city? And how could he afford to stay in a place like this?

Before he could contemplate these questions, there came a knock at the door. He spun round, panic thrumming through his body. For a moment he considered ignoring it, but then the knock came again, this time louder. He sidled up to the door, lifted the cover on the spy hole and pressed his eye to it, squinting at the distorted image of an elderly bellboy standing beside a serving trolley. The man lifted a white-gloved hand, but

Michael opened the door before he could knock a third time.

'Mr Harrison?'

'Um, yeah, that's me.'

The bellboy wheeled the serving trolley in. On top were an ice bucket and a platter with a silver lid. He stopped just inside the door and lifted the lid, allowing a puff of rich, delicious-smelling steam to swirl up from the platter. 'Your lobster thermidor, sir. Now, would you like me to open your champagne?'

Michael's stomach clenched with a sudden hunger. He had never tried lobster before, but it smelled like he'd been missing out. 'Sure,' he said. 'Why not?'

Smiling in such a forced way that it made Michael's mouth ache in sympathy, the bellboy peeled back the foil, expertly popped the cork and poured out a glass. After returning the bottle to its ice bucket, he stepped to one side and linked his hands behind his back, as if waiting for something.

'Thanks,' Michael said, still holding the door. When the man didn't budge, he realised a tip might be customary.

Letting the door swing shut, he crossed the room to a chair with an unfamiliar suit hanging on the back and checked the pockets. The only things in them were several crumpled betting slips.

'Sorry,' he said, and let out a nervous laugh. 'My wallet must be somewhere.'

He turned to inspect the room and then spotted the briefcase again. After several seconds of one-handed fumbling with the clasps, the lid popped open to reveal not a wallet, but what must have constituted several thousand dollars in used bills, stacked side-by-side.

His knees wobbled; nestled in the middle of the case was a pill bottle. He picked it up, opened the lid and looked inside. It was nearly empty, but rattling around the bottom were between ten and twenty doses of Dr Barclay's miracle drug.

'Ahem,' the bellboy said, and coughed into a clenched fist.

Michael returned the bottle to the case and plucked a ten-dollar bill from the top of a pile.

'Ten bucks?' the man said as Michael pressed it into his hand. 'You sure?'

'Yeah, why not?' Michael replied, thinking there was plenty more where it had come from.

'That's mighty kind of you, young sir.' The bellboy slid the money into his pocket and wheeled the trolley out into the hall. 'Enjoy your meal.'

'Thank you,' Michael said. 'I'm sure I will.'

3

'Michael?' a familiar voice called out in the dark. 'Can you hear me?'

Michael blinked and found himself staring up into a cloudy and starless night sky. Spots of rain dampened his face. His head hummed and throbbed like a struck gong.

Turning to one side, he discovered that he was on his back in the parking lot of the Redwood Diner. Ellis was crouched beside him, watching him from under a worry-lined brow.

Michael heaved himself up on his elbow. 'What happened? Where's Rachel?'

'I only got back a few minutes ago,' Ellis said, helping him to his feet. 'It looked like you were having a fit of some kind, so I sent her to fetch Dr Kirkwood.'

'There's no need,' Michael said. 'I'm fine, see?'

'You don't look it,' Ellis said, and released his arm.

Without support, Michael tottered. 'No, honestly, I

am,' he said, and adjusted his prosthetic, which must have twisted askew when he'd fallen. 'I usually need to rest a bit afterward. Give me five, ten minutes, I'll be good as new.'

'What, you're telling me this has happened *before*?'

'Yeah, but only a few times since—' Michael managed to stop before he mentioned his escape from Stribe Lyndhurst. 'Maybe you're right. Would it be okay if I left a little early tonight? I'll be back first thing in the morning.'

Ellis made a face like something was stuck in his throat.

'What's wrong?'

'Why don't you come inside and sit down?'

'I'm fine,' Michael repeated, annoyance creeping in. 'What is it? Just spit it out and tell me.'

'There's no easy way to say this, Michael.' Ellis lowered his gaze and raked his fingers through his hair. 'I wanted to wait until after the holidays, but I'm going to have to let you go.'

'You're *firing* me?'

'Like I said, you're a good worker, but money's tight and I need to cut overheads. I'm sorry, but I can't afford to keep an extra person on, especially someone who isn't physically fit to work. I'll pay you up until the end of the month, of course, but—'

'*Physically fit to work*?' Michael yelled, waving his prosthetic under Ellis's nose. 'What, you only just notice this?'

Ellis made that choking face again. 'I'm sorry, really I am. It's nothing personal, but I can't take the risk. What if you had a fit in the kitchen and fell on a knife? Or the hotplate, even? I got a duty as an employer, Michael. I hope you can understand.'

'Oh, I understand all right, I hear you loud and clear!'

Michael tore his apron off, hurled it at Ellis and then stomped away, voicing a string of expletives.

After a couple of hundred yards, he noticed the outline of Rachel's yellow waitress uniform bobbing toward him in the dank, drizzly night. For a moment he considered ducking into the woods to avoid the humiliation of explaining what had just happened, however this could well be the last time he ever saw her, so he forced himself to brush the tears from his cheek and waited.

It seemed to take forever, but eventually she reached him, stopped and flopped forward, her hands on her knees. 'Michael, thank god you're all right!' she spluttered between breaths. 'Dr Kirkwood wasn't home. I didn't know what else to do, so I just came back.'

'Where's Jimmy?'

'Jimmy?' She straightened up. 'He ran off as soon as you collapsed and...oh, Michael, you're crying. What happened?'

Michael rubbed furiously at his treacherous eye. 'Ellis fired me.'

'Fired you? For what?'

'Said it was because of overheads, but the real reason is he doesn't think I'm physically fit to work. Thinks I might have a seizure on the hotplate or something.'

She stepped forward and took his hand in her own. 'Let me talk to him. I bet I can get him to change his—'

'Don't bother, I can tell when I'm not wanted.'

'But where will you go? What will you do?'

Michael paused. Until then he hadn't been sure, but as if from nowhere an idea emerged in his head, already fully formed.

'San Francisco,' he said. 'There's someone I need to see.'

4

Isaac stepped into the elevator outside the Lincoln Ward and pressed the button for the ground floor. Ordinarily he enjoyed admiring his reflection in the mirrored rear wall when riding the elevator unaccompanied, however this had become an increasingly unpalatable proposition over the last few months. The mirror image now staring back at him had pale, greasy skin, dark shadows under the eyes and a forehead pocked by acne.

Letting out a shudder, he turned away. He was working too hard, and it showed. How long had it been since he'd visited his tennis club? Two months? Three, maybe? Whatever it was, he needed to get out more, to stretch his limbs, feel the sun on his face and take fresh air into his lungs. Unfortunately, between his job at the hospital and his consultancy at Bereck & Hertz Pharmaceuticals, it seemed like there was never time anymore, and as a testament his gut was beginning to overhang the waistband of his pants.

The elevator doors slid open onto the lobby of Stribe Lyndhurst Military Hospital. At this hour it was deserted, save for a dozing security guard and a cleaner sweeping fallen pine needles from under a Christmas tree in the corner. Isaac crossed the granite floor, his footsteps sending out loud, echoing claps in the expanse. Tomorrow, he and Lara would drive down to Santa Barbara to spend the holidays with his parents. It was to be the first time they met his fiancé, and in spite of his assurances that they would love her, Lara had been in a foul mood all week. Perhaps the short break and a few days without the pressures of their jobs might be just the thing they needed, although if his burgeoning waistline was anything to go by, he might have to take it easy on the trimmings this year.

Passing through the revolving doors, he emerged into a cool, overcast night and stifled a yawn. Since November, he was averaging between seventy and eighty hours in a typical working week, and Lara hadn't held back in voicing her frustrations that they weren't spending enough time together. But with Tetradyamide entering the final phase of its clinical trials, his workload had grown exponentially. The first official human trial was scheduled for early February – after Michael Humboldt's escape back in July, Isaac had decided it might be a good idea if his unofficial experiments remained off the record – and the Department of Defence hoped to begin active operations before the following year was out.

Isaac already knew what the result would be: total victory in Vietnam by the turn of 1971. Tetradyamide was an unfair advantage, improving users' speed and reaction time, and the enemy didn't stand a chance once it went into widespread circulation. The prospect of so much bloodshed made for uncomfortable thinking, particularly when the drug had potentially non-military applications as the experiments with Michael had demonstrated, but although Tetradyamide had originally been Isaac's baby, Bereck & Hertz had paid handsomely for his discovery, and what they did with it was now out of his hands.

Or at least that was what he kept telling himself.

Was this how J. Robert Oppenheimer, the so-called father of the atomic bomb and self-professed destroyer of worlds, had felt in the knowledge that soon he would be responsible for the deaths of thousands?

Trying to push the stomach-churning thought aside, Isaac made his way to the parking lot on the far the side of the hospital grounds. The wind blew slanting, abrasive rain across the path and into his face. That morning it had taken ten minutes of circling just to find an empty space, but now his car – a GTO fresh off the production line and paid for by his consultancy – stood blanketed by darkness in a lonely corner where a bulb had blown in the ring of lighting around the fence.

As he hurried toward it, a fork of lightening lit the sky. Less than two seconds passed before it was followed by an apocalyptic crash of thunder.

Isaac broke into a run, tugging his coat over his head just as the clouds above disgorged their watery load. He was thoroughly soaked by the time he reached his car. As he pulled his keys from his pocket, they slipped through his fingers, clattered onto the ground and disappeared somewhere behind the front wheel.

Tilting his head back, he shook his fist at the sky, his teeth bared as heavy raindrops pelted his face. Lara had told him she was preparing a special meal that evening, and he was already running late. At this rate they'd barely have time to exchange pleasantries in the hall before she left for her night shift.

Isaac dropped to his knees, arched his back and, suppressing the memory of a large rat he'd seen scurrying about a few days before, peered under the wheel arch. He was greeted by pitch-blackness. With no other choice, he reached out and began blindly groping behind the tyre. First his fingers brushed against something soft and soggy and then against something smooth and sharp that felt alarmingly like broken glass. Finally they came to a rest on the cactus-shaped key ring Lara had won at a fairground on their second date.

'Dr Barclay.'

Isaac was so startled by the sound of his name that he bumped his head on the side of the car and dropped his keys again. Sweeping wet hair from his face, he clambered to his feet and turned around. There was a figure in a hooded parka standing close to the fence, some thirty feet away.

'Who's there?' Isaac called, squinting through the downpour. Although the person's face was obscured, it seemed improbable any prospective mugger would address him by name.

The shadowy figure approached. When only a yard or so away, it stopped, reached up and lowered the hood.

Isaac took a step back, his breath catching in his throat. 'M-*Michael*?'

'Hello, Dr Barclay,' Michael Humboldt said, his mouth twitching into a smile. 'Bet you never thought you'd see me again.'

He was wearing a leather eye patch instead of the cotton one they'd issued him, but the difference in Michael's appearance went deeper than that. It was almost as though the burns on his face were years old instead of months. But that was counterintuitive in the absence of medical care, meaning it was probably just a trick of the light. Or, more accurately, the absence thereof.

'Michael, you came back!' Isaac exclaimed, and gave a shaky laugh. On top of his other troubles, he had been unable to shake the suspicion that, through his unauthorised testing of Tetradyamide, he was in some indirect way responsible for Michael's escape. 'I've been worried sick. The military police were looking for you, you know. They were here during the summer, asking all kinds of questions. What happened? Where have you been?'

'Flipping burgers and washing dishes, mostly.'

'Never mind,' Isaac said, his keys forgotten, 'the main thing is you're back now and we can continue where we left off with our research. Let's get you up to the Lincoln Ward. I'll find you some dry clothes and something to eat and then I can examine you properly.'

'I think not,' Michael said.

Isaac's relief was tainted by a stab of apprehension as his mind flitted back to the day Michael had tried to strangle Lara, a timely reminder that the man standing before him was potentially dangerous. He glanced over his shoulder, hoping to see someone – *anyone* – but the hospital grounds remained deserted.

'I don't get it,' he said, looking back. 'If you don't want my help, what are you doing here?'

'There's something I need, Dr Barclay,' Michael's smile had curled into something more sinister, 'and you're going to give it to me.'

5

After being fired from the Redwood Diner, Michael had returned to his boarding house, gathered up his meagre belongings, removed his savings from the tin beneath the floorboards and then walked out of Stapleton.

Over the night and following morning, he had hitch-hiked his way south, arriving in San Francisco almost five months to the day since he'd last set foot in the city. Officially AWOL since his escape, he was still a wanted man, however the vision that had come to him during his seizure the night before had changed everything, and the risks involved paled in comparison to the potential rewards.

Wearing a parka bought at a thrift shop, he'd spent the evening camped out in a bush near the perimeter of the hospital, from which he had kept a vigil over the grounds. Bit by bit the parking lot had emptied until the only car left was a flashy red Pontiac.

Just as he was finally losing hope, someone had appeared at the hospital entrance and hurried over. He'd waited until the person's identity was beyond doubt and then emerged from his hiding place, seizing his opportunity with both hands, metaphorically speaking at least.

'I...I don't understand,' Barclay stammered, panic swarming over his face like an army of ravenous ants. 'What could you possibly want from me?'

'Why, more of your miracle drug, of course.'

'*Tetradyamide*?'

'Tetradyamide, that's it! You do remember what it makes me capable of, don't you?'

Barclay rubbed the back of his neck. 'Well, I've always believed there were applications beyond simply improving speed and reaction time, although—'

'I'm not talking about reactions, Dr Barclay. I'm talking about time travel, the ability to leave my body and send my mind to a different time and place.'

'That card trick you used to pull!' Barclay took a step forward, his trepidation replaced by a sudden eagerness. 'And your escape! I always wondered about that. It wouldn't be possible unless your timing was absolutely spot-on.'

'No trick involved, just Tetradyamide. And this.' Michael turned his head to the side and tapped the scar that marked the place where shrapnel had penetrated his skull. 'Timing's an easy thing to master when you have as many do-overs as you like.'

'Your injury, of course!' Barclay exclaimed, his voice giddy and high-pitched. 'You do realise what this means, don't you? If I were able to scientifically verify what you say, it could be one of the most significant breakthroughs of the century, up there with the theory of relativity or the structure of DNA! You could—'

'What, become a caged bird again? Some sort of curio for you to conduct your experiments on? Thank you, Dr Barclay, but I think I'll pass.'

Barclay frowned, his eyebrows bunching together beneath a mop of wet hair. 'I'm sorry, Michael, but Tetradyamide is the property of Bereck & Hertz Pharmaceuticals and the United States Military now. I can't just go dishing it out to anyone who asks. And besides, since you upped and left I don't keep any in the Lincoln Ward. Apart from the latest batch at the Bereck & Hertz building, everything's already with the Department of Defence.'

Michael shook his head. Pleasurable as it was to watch this pampered, privileged man squirm, he had half-hoped it wouldn't come to this, although on some level he knew that it surely must. 'I expect the press would be extremely interested to hear about the unauthorised testing of a new drug on injured US service personnel,' he said. 'That sort of thing could do a lot of damage to an ambitious young doctor's career.'

Barclay gawped at him. 'Are you *threatening* me?'

'Call it what you want. I prefer the phrase "mutually beneficial arrangement".'

'Extortion, plain and simple!' Barclay slapped his palm against his forehead and gave a bitter laugh. 'Give you Tetradyamide or you'll ruin my career, that about the size of it?'

Michael gave a nonchalant shrug. He had no evidence to back up his claims, and it seemed doubtful any self-respecting journalist would take his word over that of a distinguished doctor, but he knew Barclay well enough from his time as a patient to guess that the man's pride might just be his weak spot.

For several seconds Barclay only glowered at him. Michael was beginning to worry that his scheme had backfired and his bluff was about to be called when at last the doctor sighed and said, 'Doesn't really look like I've got much choice then, does it?'

'No, not really.'

Barclay huffed. 'Fine then, I may have a few pills left-over upstairs. They're yours on one condition.'

'Name it.'

'If I do this then I need your word that's the end of the matter.' He took a deep breath, a fiery hatred burning in his hazel eyes. 'I never want to see or hear from you again.'

Something Michael had learned in the last few days was that one never knew what the future might hold, but he decided it to keep his own counsel. 'Hurtful as that is,' he said, 'you have my word.'

'All right then. Wait here, I'll be back in a minute.'

6

Michael squeezed through a crowded grandstand toward the line for the betting window. In the breast pocket of his second-hand suit were the remaining thirty-six dollars of his savings, plus a small glass bottle containing the eighteen (he had counted them) doses of Tetradyamide that Dr Barclay had given him the night before. It may not have seemed like many, but in theory one was all he needed to return to Stapleton before Christmas, clear Ellis's debts and sweep Rachel off her feet.

Standing at the end of the line were three girls in wide-brimmed hats and knee-length dresses. The girl on the left was wearing a blue dress and had a round, friendly face. As Michael joined behind her, she looked up, smiling, and then gasped and looked away.

He lowered his head, a familiar sinking feeling in his gut, and reached for his pocket. Without removing the bottle, he popped the lid and fumbled about until he was able to snake out a pill with his finger. Then, pretending to muffle a cough, he dropped it onto his tongue. The drug tasted every bit as bad as he remembered, and when he coughed a second time there was nothing fake about it.

As the line edged forward, he caught a glimpse of the blackboard above the betting window where the names of the horses in the first race of the day were scrawled next to their odds. Before her death, his mother had encouraged his love of reading, and for Michael's eighth birthday had bought him a book about King Arthur and the Knights of the Round Table. He had reread it over and over until the spine fell apart and the pages became loose, at which point Pa had thrown it out, ignoring his wails of complaint. The horse at the bottom of the list was called Excalibur, the name of Arthur's sword.

When it was his turn, Michael placed five bucks on Excalibur to win. Although at odds of 9-2 it was a long shot, at this stage his primary objective was to set up conditions that would be easy to alter.

Clutching his betting slip, he made his way onto the teeming balcony at the front of the grandstand. It felt uncommonly warm for December. Far below, an outer oval of dirt encircled an inner track of grass, the middle of which was given over to water features that sparkled and glistened in the morning sun. On the far side of the track, low white houses climbed a hill high into the distance.

Tilting the brim of his hat to shade his face, he wove his way through the crowds until he found a position by a metal barrier with an uninterrupted view of the starting gate. A grizzled old man with a voice like a bag of gravel offered him a filterless cigarette. Michael thanked him and smoked leaning against the railing as the horses were paraded into position.

All of a sudden a warm tingle started in his toes and danced its way up his body. The drug was taking effect, whetting his senses and giving every movement an odd, disjointed depth. Colours took on an added layer of richness. He blinked, and the crowd was perfectly silent, to a person as still as a mannequin. He blinked again, and the scene sprang back to life, regaining sound and motion.

As the last horse was led into its berth, Michael's heart quickened to a rapid *thud-thud-thud* in his chest. An expectant hush spread through the stadium. He held his breath, and then a bell rang, the gates flew open and he found himself swept up in the excitement and roaring along as loud as anyone.

The main pack started to thin by the first bend, with Excalibur, a fine-looking animal wearing number 6, close to the rear. On reaching the backstretch, even its nearest rival had pulled away, leaving clear daylight between itself and Excalibur in last place. The gap widened around the final bend, and when a sooty grey horse wearing number 2 crossed the line first, Michael's horse had only just entered the home straight.

He scrunched his betting slip into a ball and let it drop to the floor.

The old man beside him shook his head and lit another cigarette. 'Better luck next time, son.'

'You can say that again,' Michael said, and closed his eye. The darkness was immediately broken by an explosion of coloured light, then another and another, like tiny fireworks in a night sky. They flooded together to form a picture of the man's haggard face, a motionless curl of smoke unwinding from his tar-stained lips.

'Back,' Michael commanded, and the scene began to rewind. The man sucked smoke from the air, then raised a match, shook a flame into existence and used it to extinguish the ember of his cigarette. Michael's crumpled betting slip jumped off the floor and into his outstretched hand. He saw his fist clench, and when it reopened the paper was creaseless. Then his view lifted to the race-track, where he saw the horses gallop one by one back over the finishing line. As they retraced their way around the circuit, the spaces between each narrowed, until they formed a close pack and, in unison, sprang backward into the starting gate.

Michael watched himself blow life into a cigarette butt, which grew with each drag he took. When it was whole again and unlit, he handed it back to the old man, pushed away from the metal barrier, retreated through the balcony and re-entered the grandstand.

He backward-walked to the betting window, span on his heel and swapped his betting slip for a five-dollar bill with the clerk.

'Go.'

The scene ground to a halt and then leapt forward again, the arrow of time inverting like the needle of a compass placed next to a magnet.

'Good morning,' the clerk said. 'What'll it be?'

Michael took a step back and glanced at the black-board above the window. The horse wearing 2 was called Wild Child.

He stepped forward again and pulled out his narrow roll of cash. 'Everything on Wild Child,' he said, laying it on the counter.

'Certainly, sir.' The clerk took his money, licked her thumb and stacked the bills into piles of different numeration. 'So, that's thirty-six dollars on number two to win,' she said, passing him a new betting slip. 'Good luck, and have a nice day.'

Michael stepped away from the window and closed his eye. 'Now,' he said.

There was a whoosh like a blast of air from a passing truck. He opened his eye again, blinking in the bright sunshine. He was back on the balcony. Far below, Wild Child was being paraded, the jockey upright in his stir-rups, waving to the crowd.

Suddenly someone slapped Michael on the back. He looked round to see the smoker at the metal barrier smiling up at him.

'Congratulations, son. Must be your lucky day!'

Michael glanced down the betting slip in his hand, which clearly displayed the name Wild Child at odds of 4-1. 'Yeah,' he said, smiling back, 'guess it must be.'

7

Michael sat perched on the rim of a bathtub that was more like a small swimming pool and ran the gold-plated taps. His suite at The Fairmont Hotel cost fifty bucks a night, but was worth every cent. The bathroom was tiled with slabs of flecked marble, each roughly the size of his torso. For some unknown reason there were two basins in the sink, plus a knee-high one next to the can which the elderly bellboy – the same man from his vision in the parking lot of the Redwood Diner – had called a 'bidet' when showing him around last night. On the glass shelf below the mirror, a row of miniature bottles had been arranged in a line. He selected one marked *Bubble Bath*, unscrewed the lid and held it to his nose. The scented gel reminded him of the smell of the hairdressers where his mother had worked part-time until she became too sick to leave the house, so he poured half into the water, returned to the bedroom and ordered the bacon and eggs, blueberry pancakes, coffee and a freshly squeezed orange juice from the room service menu.

Back in the bathroom, he wiped away a circle of steam from the mirror, wet a cotton ball and set about cleaning his hollow eye socket as the bath filled.

There had been six races in total yesterday, and he had bet on each and won, using a single dose of Tetradyamide to turn thirty-eight dollars into a shade under ten thousand. After that the drinks had flowed free of charge at the racetrack bar, which made little sense since it was the first time in his life he could afford to buy them. Everyone there wanted to be his friend, or so it had seemed. Strangers, who a day before might have flinched at the sight of him, had instead offered warm smiles and hearty handshakes.

As the combination of Tetradyamide and alcohol lowered his inhibitions and loosened his tongue, Michael had begun to revel in the attention. At the end of the evening, the girl in the blue dress had approached him, twirling her hair and fluttering her eyelids as she spoke, as though the briefcase full of money he was clutching somehow masked the scars on his face. At that point Michael's thoughts had immediately turned to Rachel, and with a worsening headache as the effects of the drug diminished, he made his excuses and caught a cab, instructing the driver to take him to The Fairmount.

He'd paid for his room in cash and then, once the bellboy had shown him around, ordered the lobster thermidor (what else?) and a bottle of Champagne from room service. It tasted so good that he had ordered a second serving, devoured that too and then collapsed on the bed in his underwear, where he had remained for ten straight hours before waking five minutes ago with a mild hangover.

Once the tub was full, he stripped off and dipped a precautionary toe into the water. It was hot – almost too hot – but he lowered himself in all the same, drawing a sharp breath that he only released once his shoulders were submerged. With the sound of bubbles crackling in his ears, he leaned back and closed his eye.

His plan had come off without a hitch. After breakfast, he would check out of the hotel, do some shopping and once suitably attired, possibly with a glass eye if he could find one, catch a bus back to Stapleton, where he would show Rachel his winnings, tell her how he truly felt and at long last begin their life together. Soon enough, all would be right with the world.

Michael must have drifted off to that comforting thought, because the next thing he knew the bathwater was tepid and the bubbles on the surface had dissolved away, leaving a soapy film in their place. The sound of someone knocking on the door was coming from the bedroom.

He climbed out, wrapped a dressing gown around his dripping, water-shrivelled body and then hurried to answer the door. The bellboy was standing on the other side beside a serving trolley holding two silver platters, a glass of orange juice, a pot of coffee and a folded copy of *The Daily Californian*.

Michael instructed him to leave the food on the table by the balcony doors and plucked the newspaper from the trolley as the man wheeled it past. He was confronted by a grainy photograph of himself shaking hands with the racetrack manager under the headline, *Brave Handicapped Man Wins Big!* All of a sudden his bare feet seemed to lose traction with the floor and he felt himself slipping. He grabbed a hold of the doorframe, his fingernails digging indentations in the wood.

This was bad. Very bad.

The bellboy finished setting the table and stepped to one side, hands tucked behind his back expectantly.

'Get out!' Michael yelled. 'Out, *now*!'

'But—'

Michael grabbed him by the collar, twisted him round and propelled him through the open door and into the hall.

'M-my trolley,' the man spluttered.

Cursing, Michael turned back and retrieved the empty trolley. As he wheeled it out after the bellboy, the dial above the elevator at the end of the hall reached 4 – the floor they were standing on. There was a soft chime and then the doors slid open. Two stony-faced men stepped out, both in the olive-green uniforms and black helmets of the military police.

Michael's stomach leapt so high that it felt like it was trying to climb his throat and exit his body through his mouth. As he reached for the door handle, the officer on the left glanced up. The man had a straight-edged moustache and a copy of *The Daily Californian* tucked under his arm. The tag on his shirt read *CPT MAYER*.

'Private Humboldt?'

Michael tried to close the door, but it struck the side of the trolley and deflected back open, and a second later Mayer had barged the bellboy out of the way and was forcing his way in.

'I can explain,' Michael said, taking a step back.

'Save it for the court martial,' the second officer said as he followed Mayer into the room. He was stocky, with a swarthy complexion and a squashed nose that looked like it had been busted several times over. The name on his tag read *CPL GARCIA*.

Michael glanced over his shoulder. His briefcase was lying at the end of the bed next to his detached prosthetic, the bottle of Tetradyamide nestled somewhere among his winnings. Turning back, he saw Garcia move toward him, a hairy hand on the baton swinging from his belt. Before Garcia could get any closer, Michael rabbit-punched him in the Adam's apple. He let out a noise like a punctured air mattress and crumpled.

Michael didn't see him hit the floor; he was already diving toward the bed. He landed someway short and skidded, the dressing gown riding up around his thighs and the carpet burning raw strips on his elbows and knees. As he scrambled for the briefcase like a rabid, three-legged dog, a steel toecap slammed into his exposed private parts, and he collapsed face-first, a fingertip resting on the handle.

Mayer stepped into view and lowered himself to his haunches. Using the tip of his baton, he lifted the lid of the briefcase and emitted a low whistle. 'Looks like you've got some explaining to do, Private Humboldt.'

Chapter III

Metamorphosis

1

Michael lay on a bare wooden cot, his head bloodied and bruised. Following his arrest at The Fairmount, his captors had at least spared him the indignity of being dragged through the lobby in a bathrobe and had allowed him time to dress before escorting him out of the hotel and into the back of a waiting jeep. That was their only act of generosity, as they had then driven him to a military base near Fairfax, led him to an empty holding cell and, once the door was closed and there was no one about to witness it, dished out a beating that would have made Pa proud, were he still alive. Michael had tried appealing to their sense of reason, but it didn't matter that he had been injured in the line of duty, nor that his escape had taken place on US soil: desertion was desertion as far as Mayer and Garcia were concerned, and he was a coward, even lower than a cockroach.

An endless cycle of anger, frustration and regret had played in a loop around Michael's brain in the four hours he'd already spent festering in his cell. Right about now he should have been waiting for a bus back to Humboldt County, ready to sweep Rachel off her feet before embarking on a lifetime of first-class travel and luxury hotels, but thanks to his recklessness at the racetrack yesterday, he instead faced incarceration at the base until a date for his court martial could be fixed.

What had become of his briefcase, he could only wonder. If Mayer's hungry expression back at the hotel had been anything to go by, Michael very much doubted the money would ever make it to the man's superiors. The fool probably didn't even realise the most valuable thing the case contained was not the ten-thousand dollars but the near-empty bottle of pills. If the military ever got wind of what they were, Michael figured Dr Barclay could end up facing a court martial too. The thought made him smirk, but his satisfaction was hollow; his pills were gone, and with Barclay also facing time behind bars, so was any hope of gaining further access to Tetradyamide. Having only fleetingly tasted what might have been, Michael had lost everything, including the chance to undo his initial mistake.

Choking back a sob, he removed his suit jacket and positioned it under his head to form a makeshift pillow. It did little to cushion the wooden slats, and after another uncomfortable minute or two spent staring at the raw brickwork of the ceiling, he sat up and tried folding the jacket over on itself to increase its thickness. That was when he noticed a small, hard lump in the material. Frowning, he went through his pockets one by one. Since he'd been forced to turn them out on arriving at the base, they were all empty, but as his fingers explored the lining of the breast pocket, he detected a small hole in the stitching. Tugging at a loose thread, he widened the gap and slid his index finger in. It brushed against something small, round and sticky.

A silent gasp escaped Michael's lips. He pulled the pill out and picked off the fluff. Tetradyamide: a single dose. It must have fallen out when he'd opened the bottle at the racetrack yesterday. Such a stroke of good fortune when he needed it most could only be fate, singling him out and intervening to grant him one last chance. But that was all he needed, and he swallowed the pill down, hardly noticing the taste.

Several minutes passed, and then a wide grin spread across his face as a light, fluttery sensation branched out from his stomach and spread through his body.

Footsteps echoed in the corridor, stopping in front of his cell. The grate on the door slid back to reveal Corporal Garcia, the most enthusiastic participant in Michael's earlier beating.

'Lunch is served.' Garcia raised a dented tin plate of rehydrated eggs into view, cleared his throat and let a thick, green-specked loogie dribble onto it. 'Special sauce,' he explained, 'reserved just for deserters.'

'I'll kill you,' Michael said.

'Huh?'

'You hard of hearing or something? I. Will. Kill. You.'

Garcia's ugly face creased into an even uglier grin. 'Want another piece of me, do ya?'

Michael shrugged his shoulders benignly.

'Okay, buster, you got it.'

Garcia unlocked the door, pushed it open and entered. Striding across the cell, he tossed the plate to the floor and reached out to seize Michael by the neck. The action seemed slow and jerky, like watching the individual frames of a movie unfold at half-speed, and was so thoroughly predictable that Michael had plenty of time to duck and roll off the cot, leaving his assailant clutching at thin air. Off balance, Garcia toppled over and struck his forehead against the wall behind the cot.

Michael was immediately on his feet. Stepping forward, he unhooked the baton from Garcia's belt.

'What the hell!' Garcia spun around, his mouth open. 'How'd you move so fast?'

'Must be a trick of the light,' Michael replied, and swung the baton down on top of the man's head. There was a satisfying crunch, like a saucer crushed in a towel, and Garcia slumped onto the cot. Smiling, Michael raised the baton and brought it down again and again, only stopping when the bricks of the wall were spotted with blood.

'Told you I'd kill you,' he said, and let the baton slip from his fingers.

Garcia lay motionless, an arm curled awkwardly under his body and a sightless eye directed up at the ceiling.

Letting out a deep, contented sigh, Michael stepped through the open door of his cell and began up a corridor lined with flaky, yellowing paint. He hadn't gone far when he heard the thunder of approaching boots. Hurrying back the way he'd come, he passed his cell again and rounded the corner at the opposite end of the corridor.

'Garcia!' someone behind him shouted. 'That deserting son-of-a-bitch got Garcia!'

Michael turned another corner and then another before eventually finding his path blocked by a dead end. He was trapped, and the thudding of heavy boots was getting closer. Turning so his back was to the wall, he saw Mayer round the corner with his baton drawn, his face a mask of irrepressible rage and another two baton-wielding military police officers close on his heels.

Michael held up his hand, which, he now saw, was streaked with Garcia's blood. It was the brightest shade of red he'd ever seen, as if all other variations of the colour were cheap imitations of this purest form. With Tetradyamide in his veins, he was all-powerful, a king in the making, and there was nothing they could do to stop him. A bubble of energy rose through his body, passing out and beyond him as a wave that rolled along the walls of the corridor toward his pursuers. He closed his eye, and a thousand arrows of coloured light struck his retina in the same instant, fusing together to form the image of Captain Mayer frozen in midstride, his teeth gritted and his baton raised.

'Back,' Michael said, and Mayer and his companions were swept away and out of sight.

He saw himself turn to face the wall, then retrace his steps down the corridor, passing his cell before doubling back and entering. As he backed up to Garcia's body, a bloodied baton rolled across the floor and launched itself into his hand. He watched himself swing it over and over, each blow repairing the caved-in head until it was whole once more.

As the now-living Garcia heaved himself up, Michael felt a pang of remorse that his sweet vengeance had been so temporary, and then the backward-playing images sped up to the point that all detail was lost in an ever-changing flurry of shape and colour.

He waited patiently, focusing on the time before his arrest as the recent past unwound before him in a blur. Eventually the images slowed, and he found himself being manhandled from a jeep outside The Fairmont Hotel, his cuts and bruises erased.

With shocked guests looking on, Mayer and Garcia backward-marched him through the foyer and into a waiting elevator. Back on the good old fourth floor, they steered him to his hotel suite, released him and stepped back as he stripped and then covered his nakedness with a bathrobe. Barking silent orders, they forced him flat on the floor. Mayer deposited the briefcase against the end of the bed, at which point Garcia collapsed, clutching his neck. All of a sudden Michael slid back across the carpet, launched into the air and then turned to punch the rising Garcia in the Adam's apple. His captors retreated into the hall and past a shocked-looking bellboy, who then stepped in to clear Michael's untouched breakfast from the table before wheeling it out on a trolley.

Michael watched himself close the door and back into the bathroom, where he took his robe off, slid into the tub and closed his eye.

'Go,' he said and blinked.

Suddenly a layer of bubbles was bobbing around his chin, the water now hot against his skin.

'Not a moment to lose,' he muttered and clambered out.

Without bothering to dry himself, he raced from the bathroom, his wet feet skidding over the floor. After hurriedly attaching his prosthetic, he pulled on his clothes and snatched up his briefcase.

As he stepped from his suite, he caught sight of the elderly bellboy pushing a trolley out of the elevator. He turned in the opposite direction, paced toward the emergency stairwell at the far end of the hall and slipped through the door, holding it open a crack to peek back out. The bellboy had stopped outside his room and was knocking on the door.

Michael held his breath and waited. After a while the bellboy shrugged and began wheeling the trolley back toward the elevator, just as the dial above the doors reached 4 and Mayer and Garcia stepped out, guffawing at the punchline of some unheard joke. They stopped the bellboy, who nodded, pointed toward Michael's room and then, leaving his trolley where it was, pulled out a bunch of keys and opened it for them.

As the three men disappeared into the empty suite, Michael finally let the door to the stairwell swing shut. He descended to the ground floor and strolled out through the lobby and into bright sunshine of a clear winter's morning. There was a jeep parked up outside with the letters MP stencilled on the hood. After a quick glance about to check there was no one looking, he crouched beside it and punctured the front tyre with the hook of his prosthetic.

Smiling, he drew himself up and mouthed the word, 'Now.'

2

As Michael blinked, the scene around him shifted and changed like someone had spliced unconnected frames into a showreel. The grand exterior of The Fairmount Hotel was snapped out in an instant, replaced by the indifferent face of a gum-chewing woman in a Greyhound kiosk. A light breeze blew against his skin, ruffling the material of a tailored suit that was infinitely more handsome than the thrift-shop one he'd bought for his day at the races. He glanced down to see his briefcase dangling loosely from the fingers of his left hand and immediately tightened his grip on the handle.

It had worked: he was a free man again, and his plan was back on track.

'Where to, hun?' the woman asked.

Michael stepped back and looked about. He was standing on a sidewalk with a row of stationary buses along the curb behind him. The engine of the nearest idled while a short line of passengers filed aboard. A placard behind the windscreen read *EUREKA, HUM-BOLDT CO.*

He turned back to the kiosk, catching a glimpse of his reflection in the window. On top of his new suit there was a further piece of evidence supporting the notion that, in this timeline, he had spent the morning shopping: in place of his eye patch was a glass eye so realistic it took him a moment to realise that was what it was.

He winked at his reflection and muttered, 'Looking *good.*'

'What's that, hun?'

'Nothing. When does the Eureka bus leave?'

'Ten minutes.' The woman blew a large, pink bubble, let it pop and then sucked the torn strands back in. 'You want a single or a return?'

'A single,' Michael told her. 'I'm only going one way.'

3

Michael lurked in the shadows, his briefcase held by his side and a bunch of tulips tucked under his arm. It was Sunday evening, but this close to Christmas the diner was relatively busy. Looking through the window, he could see Ellis behind the hatch to the kitchen, his head and shoulders bobbing as he flipped burgers on the hotplate. Rachel was nowhere to be seen, and in her place an ungainly new waitress circled the tables with all the grace of a rhinoceros.

Michael gritted his teeth: it made a mockery of what Ellis had said about money being tight, and his sense of longing for the place where he'd passed so many happy hours was soured, his firing clearly having more to do with Ellis witnessing his seizure than the need to cut overheads.

All of a sudden the door opened and Mr Sykes stumbled out, his hands deep in the pockets of his coat. Michael ducked behind a dumpster, hoping he hadn't been spotted. He heard Mr Sykes sneeze, followed by a groan of rusty hinges and then the splutter of a worn-out engine coughing into life, and a moment later a car rolled into view before turning onto the road.

Michael waited until the taillights were swallowed up by the night. As he drew himself up, it dawned on him that Sunday was Rachel's day off. Shaking his head at his forgetfulness, he turned away and began up the roadside in the same direction as Mr Sykes's car, retracing the path he had walked after every shift at the diner.

It took a little under fifteen minutes to reach the other side of Stapleton, where Rachel and her father shared a rickety old wooden house set next to a small orchard of bare-branched apple trees. A weathervane in the shape of a rooster spun on the ridge of the roof.

Michael approached, half-wishing he had something better to offer than the now-wilted flowers he'd bought when the bus had stopped for gas that afternoon. Not that it mattered, of course; the money in his case had the potential to solve all their problems, perhaps even his fractured relationship with Ellis.

He climbed onto the porch, walked past a swing chair creaking gently on its chains and opened the mesh screen on the door. After a brief pause to flatten his suit, he gave a tentative knock.

Thirty second passed, then sixty, and still no one answered. He knocked again and took a step back. The lights were on but he saw no hint of movement inside. Aside from the diner, there were few options in town by way of entertainment on a Sunday night, but it was possible Rachel had gone to neighbouring Lausanne, where he remembered her saying she had a friend.

With a weary sigh, he turned away and began back down the steps from the porch. It looked like he'd have to wait until morning and try again. Fortunately, though, he'd said nothing to his landlady on leaving the boarding house three nights ago, so there was every chance his room would be waiting just as he'd left it. Either way, the temperature was dropping, and there didn't seem much point—

'Michael, is that you?'

He turned to see Rachel silhouetted against the light of the open door, the shape of her slender body discernible through the thin material of her nightgown. Her hair was tussled like she'd been sleeping.

'Rachel! Did I wake you? I don't even know what time it is.'

'What are you doing here?' she asked, a distance to her voice that he'd never detected before.

'I didn't think anyone was home,' he said, climbing back onto the porch and holding the tulips out. 'Here, I got these for you.'

She frowned as he pushed the sagging flowers into her hand. 'Gee, I...um, I don't know what to say. *Wait*, is that a glass eye? And where did you get those clothes?'

'You like?' Michael asked, squeezing past her and into the house. He laid his briefcase on the kitchen table and began opening the clasps. 'I bought them with this.'

Rachel remained by the door, gently rocking on the heels of her bare feet. 'Michael, I really don't think you should be here. It's late, you know, and now's really not a good—'

'Please, don't say anything yet! There's something I need to show you first.' He opened the case and stepped back.

She clapped her free hand over her mouth. 'Where *did* you get all that?' she whispered through her fingers, her eyes fixed on the case. 'Please don't tell me you've done something stupid, Michael.'

'No, it's nothing like that,' he said, pulling her trembling hand from her mouth and linking his fingers with hers. 'I won it, fair and square. It's mine. Or ours, I mean. Nearly ten-thousand dollars, all told. Don't you see, Rachel? We can leave Stapleton in the morning. I've got it all figured out, we'll fly to Europe, Italy first – you've always wanted to see Venice, haven't you? – then Paris, the city of love. We'll ditch this joint and travel the world together. It's what you always talked about.'

'You won it? B-but how?'

'It's complicated. Look, there's a lot about me I haven't told you yet. For one thing, my name isn't Harrison, it's Humboldt.'

'*Humboldt*? You're kidding, right?'

'Yeah, I know, weird coincidence. Not that I believe in coincidences anymore. I hated not being honest with you about it, but, believe me, I had good reason. What I'm trying to tell you is that I can do something special, something no one else can do.' He reached into the case, pulled out his bottle of Tetradyamide and gave it a little shake. 'With these pills, I can win any bet I place. The money in this case is just the tip of the iceberg.'

She didn't say anything but just stood there, staring down at his winnings and looking like the slightest of breezes might blow her over.

This certainly wasn't how Michael had envisioned things going, so he decided to cut to the chase. 'What I came here to say, Rachel, is that I love you. Have since the first moment I saw you outside the diner, in fact. Ever since that day, all I've wanted is to make you happy, to give you all the things you talked about, and this is my chance to do that.' He took a deep breath. 'Listen, I know

I might not be much to look at, but what do you say? Me and you, how about it?'

His proposition was answered by the bathroom door swinging open. Jimmy Peltzer walked out, bare-chested beneath his open shirt. He stopped in his tracks, looked up and then drew his lips back in a broken-toothed grin.

'The freak! What the hell are *you* doin' back in town, freakshow?'

Michael glanced desperately to Rachel, praying for any explanation apart from the obvious. She just slid her hand from his and, gazing down at the floor, muttered, 'You shouldn't have come here.'

Suddenly he saw that his hopes and dreams had been built on foundations of sand, and were now disintegrating around him. He imagined her with Jimmy, their sweaty, naked bodies entwined, writhing in the darkness, and in that moment something inside of him sagged and then snapped, something so tender and fragile that it could never be fixed.

Buttoning his fly, Jimmy took a step closer. 'I asked you a question, freak. What you doin' here?'

'I...I must have made a mistake,' Michael said, his voice no more than a whisper.

'Damn right you did.' All of a sudden Jimmy noticed the flowers in Rachel's hand. 'Aw, hell! You didn't think...*what*, you and Rachel? *Seriously*?' He began to laugh, an ugly, bass rumbling.

Michael returned the pill bottle to his briefcase and closed the lid, his shame complete. 'I think I'd better be going now.'

'Whoa, hold on just a second!' Jimmy said. 'What you got there?'

Michael's skin began to prickle with a fiery heat. He drew the case to his chest. 'That's none of your concern, Jimmy. Like you said, I got it all wrong.'

'Leave him be,' Rachel said, suddenly emerging from her trance-like state and stepping between them. 'What difference does it make? Michael said he's going, didn't he?'

Jimmy shouldered past her and moved to block the way to the door. 'The case, freak. Hand it over.'

'No.'

Jimmy snarled and shoved Michael in the chest, sending him staggering backward into the sink. The briefcase slipped from Michael's hand. As it hit the floor, the lid flew open and a landslide of cash cascaded out.

For a second Jimmy could only gawp. Then, slowly, the gears of his greedy brain began to turn. He reached back to a checked hunting jacket hanging behind the door (how had Michael failed to notice that?) and pulled out the same pearl-handled revolver he'd been carrying that night at the diner.

'So,' he said, pointing it at Michael, 'are you man enough to finish what you start this time, or are you just gonna collapse again?'

Michael stole a final glance at Rachel, but she couldn't even meet his eye. 'Okay, Jimmy,' he said. 'You win.'

'Yeah, that's what I thought.'

4

Michael sat gently sobbing into the crook of his arm among the jumble of rusty garden tools, disassembled lawnmower parts and half-empty paint tins at the back of Ellis's shed. Just under an hour ago, he had been the returning hero, ready to sweep Rachel off her feet and whisk her away, so full of pride and hope for the future. But in the space of the few short minutes he'd spent inside the house that well had run dry, never again to be replenished. Now he had lost everything: not only his beloved, but also his winnings and the bottle of Tetradyamide.

How could he have been so stupid? Had he really believed she could ever love him back, that her feelings for him ran any deeper than tolerance and sympathy? They were in there now, Jimmy and her, probably laughing at his expense as they counted his cash and worked out how to spend it.

Michael began to tremble as another bout of sobbing shook his body. He should have died in Vietnam, or during one of his failed suicide attempts back at Stribe Lyndhurst, but fate had kept him alive only to taunt him. There was nothing left for him in this cruel, heartless world, but never mind; right here and now he could finish the job started back in the jungle ten months ago.

He staggered to his feet and grasped the handle of a pitchfork leaned up against the wall, sending the cobweb-tangled collection of shovels, hoes and rakes stacked alongside it clattering to the floor. Positioning it upside-down, he leaned forward, letting the prongs dig into the soft underbelly of his neck. His weight finely balanced on the balls of his feet, all he needed was to edge forward and gravity would do the work, bringing an end to the life of Michael Humboldt.

With Pa now rotting in the ground like Eugene and Michael's mother before him, there would be no one left to mourn Michael's passing. In fact, apart from Rachel and Jimmy, nobody even knew he was back in Stapleton. It being winter, his body could very well remain in the shed for days, weeks or until the smell grew so bad that Ellis eventually came to investigate.

But no: this was not how the story ended. Michael was a survivor, and he would give neither Jimmy nor Rachel the satisfaction of walking away from what was rightfully his. The injury that had bestowed his ability to send his

mind through time was a gift, not a curse. It was what
separated him from ordinary men. It was what made him
superior and, having already defeated the odds to recover
his case once that day, he would just have to do it again.

As he withdrew the pitchfork from under his chin, he
heard a faint whistling outside the shed. For a moment he
thought it was only the wind, but the sound grew steadily
louder until there could be no mistake. Using the
pitchfork for support, he clambered over the debris-
strewn floor and peered through the gap in the door. The
clouds had parted, making way for the moon to pour its
milky light onto the path leading down to the road. All of
a sudden Jimmy strolled by, swinging Michael's briefcase
gaily by his side, a smug grin on his face and a bounce in
his step like he hadn't a care in the world.

Michael's mind immediately catapulted back to his
escape from a military prison cell, replaying the moment
he had caved in Corporal Garcia's head with the man's
own baton. Although, through his later actions, that deed
now existed only in his memory, the look on Garcia's
face had been priceless, and there was no denying the
thrill that Michael had felt at taking a life. Except this
time, in his mind's eye, it wasn't Garcia's face that he
saw staring up at him in terror, but Jimmy's, and in that
instant he knew what he must do.

Pushing open the door, he stepped outside, the
pitchfork clutched by his side. Jimmy was about ten feet
away by now, so he hurried after at a trot, calling out,
'Hey, Jimmy!'

Jimmy spun around, his eyes bulging as he took in
Michael's rapid approach with the pitchfork held out like
a spear. For an instant he didn't move, and then he
nudged back his coat and dropped his hand to his pistol.
His fingers had barely brushed the grip before Michael

drove the prongs into his chest, running him through. Surprising it was, the lack of resistance.

Jimmy opened his mouth and produced a rasping cough that showered Michael's face with specks of blood, then toppled backward onto the path. His arms and legs twitched briefly before going limp.

Michael stooped to reach for the dead man's gun, dropped it in his pocket and then retrieved his case. 'Sorry Jimmy, but I changed my mind,' he said, straightening up. 'Looks like you lose instead.'

Jimmy lay motionless, a dark circle of blood spreading out from his body.

Michael had done it: the pills were his once more, and he would never again be parted from Tetradyamide. No more would he let other people walk all over him; a new chapter was beginning in his life, one in which he would not be held back by sentimentality. From here on he was only out for Number One.

Turning back to the house, he saw that the lights were on in one of the upstairs bedrooms. Rachel was standing by the window. As she saw Michael watching her, she turned to flee, letting the drapes fall shut.

He began back up the path. There was still one task to complete.

Chapter IV

A Decade in its Final Throes

1

Isaac stood in front of the bathroom mirror and fumbled with the knot of his bow tie. No matter how many times he'd seen his dad tie one, for some reason he had never been able to master the technique himself. Grudgingly he admitted defeat, pulled the pesky thing from his collar and tossed it to the floor. He was already running late for the Stribe Lyndhurst New Year's bash, so he returned to the bedroom and rummaged through his drawers until he located the clip-on he'd last worn on his graduation from medical school.

Back in the bathroom and with the clip-on secured around his neck, he wet a comb and began to sweep back his hair, when suddenly his blood ran cold. Protruding from the left side of his head was a grey hair. He lowered the comb and, suppressing an involuntary gag reflex, leaned in toward the mirror for a closer look. The offending strand was a couple of inches in length and curly and wiry in texture, jutting out perpendicular to the rest of his sleek, jet-black locks. Isaac couldn't quite believe his eyes; he wouldn't even turn thirty until next summer, so such a premature sign of aging could only be the result of the recent stress he'd been under.

In retrospect, he could see that he'd handled the Michael Humboldt situation badly. Christmas with Lara at his parents' place in Santa Barbara was supposed to be a break from the pressures of their jobs, but instead had been fraught with anxiety. Lara and his mom had gotten along famously, but, unable to shake the incident in the hospital parking lot from his thoughts, Isaac had brought his old notebook – the only record of his experiments with Michael earlier that year – hidden in the dust jacket of Gray's Anatomy, and had reread his observations several times over in the small hours while the rest of the house slept.

Although it went against both common sense and established scientific consensus, there was now little doubt in his mind that Michael might truly be capable of the things he claimed. It was a lot to get one's head around, but according to relativity there was no such thing as absolute time, only a separate dimension in four-dimensional Spacetime. And although it might not be possible to move physically backward and forward through time as one did through space, might not the brain injury Michael had sustained in Vietnam have somehow altered the way in which Tetradyamide affected him, allowing his consciousness to flit between two unconnected moments in much the way a physical object could theoretically pass through a wormhole and emerge at a distant point in space?

Isaac let out a sigh, clasped the grey hair between his thumb and forefinger, plucked it from his scalp and then washed it down the plughole. However intriguing the hypothesis was, if he never saw Michael Humboldt again it would be too soon.

On returning to the bedroom, he pulled on the pair of black oxfords Lara had left polished and neatly positioned at the foot of the bed. The party would be in full swing by now, and by the time he reached the banqueting hall she would have been waiting close to an hour. Perhaps he should stop for a gift on his way, something gushy and romantic. But then again it was unlikely he'd find anywhere open at this time on New Year's Eve, and further delay would only increase the trouble he was already in.

He pulled his tuxedo jacket on and hurried down the hall, pausing to scoop up his keys. As he reached for the door handle, there was a knock on the other side. It was probably Mrs Riley, the lonely old crone from two doors down who took in stray cats and actively sought to engage Isaac and Lara in pointless and repetitive conversation almost every time they left the apartment.

Smiling over gritted teeth, he opened the door. 'Mrs Riley, it's nice of you to stop by, but—'

Instead of his elderly neighbour, he was confronted by a man in a fedora hat, sunshades and a cream trench coat with the collar turned up. 'M-*Michael*?' he stammered, taking a step back.

'The very same.' Michael Humboldt rested his briefcase on the floor and removed his shades. In addition to an obviously fake eye, the colour of which didn't quite match the tone of his real one, something had changed in his appearance, a tightening of his features that lent his face a newly threatening quality. 'You're looking very smart, Dr Barclay,' he said. 'Going someplace special?'

Isaac slid the individual keys on his key ring between the gaps between his fingers to form an impromptu knuckleduster. Michael might have successfully called his bluff once, but there would be no repeat performance. 'What do you want now?' he demanded, tensing his arm. 'And how did you find out where I live?'

Michael glanced down at the keys in Isaac's hand and then looked up with a sorry shake of his head. 'Really, Dr Barclay, I had hoped violence wouldn't be necessary. And your address is listed in the phone book. I've already visited an Ian Barclay and an Immanuel, but you were third on the list.'

Isaac glared at him, his rage spilling over. 'You lied, Michael! You promised we'd never see each other again. You said that once I gave you what you wanted that would be the end of it!'

'Yes, I do apologise, but my circumstances have since changed.'

Isaac took a deep breath. Much as he wanted rid of this unwelcome guest, he needed to keep his cool or risk drawing the attention of his neighbours. Perhaps a threat of his own might do the trick.

'Listen,' he said, drawing his shoulders back, 'whatever you're selling, I'm not buying this time. Go ahead and go to the press if you want, we'll see who they believe.' He took another step back and lifted the receiver of the telephone on the hall table. 'I'm calling the police, and I suggest you're some-where else when they arrive.'

'I wouldn't do that if I were you.'

'No? And why's that?'

Michael reached into his pocket and pulled out a revolver with a pearl handle. As he raised it and drew back the hammer, Isaac's bladder loosened and a trickle of warm urine slid down his leg.

2

Isaac parked up outside the Bereck & Hertz building, killed the engine and then withdrew his keys from the ignition. Looking down at the cactus-shaped key ring, he imagined Lara waiting angry and alone at a party he'd never make. He scoured his mind, desperate for another way out, but it appeared that he had little choice but to go along with Michael's demands if he ever wanted see her again.

'I've got to ask,' he said, turning in his seat, 'what's with the getup?'

'What, this? It's meant to be inconspicuous.'

'I'm not sure it's working, Michael. Sunshades after dark? I mean come on, really, are you *trying* to look like a B-movie spy?'

Michael scowled, his cheeks flushing with colour. 'Quit stalling,' he growled, but removed his glasses again all the same. 'Let's go.'

Isaac shook his head. 'There's round-the-clock security. They won't let you in. Why don't you wait here and I'll bring it down to you?'

'You think I'm letting you go in by yourself?' Michael clicked his tongue against the roof of his mouth, lifted the gun from his lap and trained it on Isaac's chest. 'Much as I'd like to believe otherwise, Dr Barclay, you'll only run if I let you out of my sight. Come now, a resourceful fellow like you, I'm sure you'll think of something.'

Isaac gripped the steering wheel and stared up through the windshield at the mirrored windows of the thirty-storey office block. 'I'll come straight back,' he said. 'You have my word.'

'No, that won't do.' The gun wavered momentarily in Michael's hand as he leaned over to open the driver's door with the hook of his prosthetic arm and then settled on Isaac's chest again. 'Like I told you, we're going in together. It's not like you've got a choice.'

Isaac stared down the barrel of the gun, then up into Michael's cold, unflinching face. What he had suspected was a trick of the light could no longer be denied: something had changed in the patient he'd treated five months earlier. It seemed as though Michael's burns had healed abnormally fast, giving them the appearance of a childhood injury as opposed to one less than a year in the past. Had Isaac's life not been on the line, he might have been consumed by professional curiosity.

'Fine, have it your way,' he said, and climbed out of the car.

'That's better.' Michael slid the gun into his pocket, passed Isaac his briefcase and followed him out.

The effect of gravity seemed to have trebled as Isaac climbed the steps to the front of the Bereck & Hertz building, making every stair a battle of mind over body. Some overpaid but untalented interior designer had decided to clad the foyer in stained pine and decorated it with light fittings comprised of reindeer antlers, creating the overall impression of a mountain lodge crash-landed in the heart of urban California. The security guard on the front desk was Frank: middle-aged and overweight, with a penchant for processed meat that suggested his ticker didn't have too many miles left on the clock.

As they approached, Frank lowered the strip of beef jerky he'd been chewing and knotted his shaggy eyebrows together. 'Dr Barclay, what are you doing back here? Thought you'd be out celebrating like everybody else.'

Isaac shifted Michael's briefcase to his other hand and glanced at the clock on the wall: only fifty-five minutes of the decade remained. Lara would be beyond livid by now.

'Everybody with a normal job, Frank,' he said, and attempted a chuckle. 'Looks like you and I get the bum deals.'

'You can say that again!' Frank leaned back in his chair, his gut straining the buttons of his uniform. 'Still, the entire building's closed until Monday. Not a soul here 'part from me.'

'That's okay,' Isaac said and glanced at Michael, who was standing at his shoulder with the gun forming an ominous bulge in his coat pocket. 'This here is, uh, Professor Bergstrom, visiting from Stockholm University. He's a leading expert in the field of Neurochemistry and has been kind enough to look over a paper I've been working on.'

At the bogus introduction, Michael smiled and dipped his head.

'That so?' Frank asked, eying him with suspicion. 'Looks a little young for a professor, if you ask me. You speaka da English, pal?'

'Fluently,' Michael replied.

Isaac gave another nervous chuckle. 'The Swedish education system puts our own to shame, unfortunately. Over there it's not unusual for academics to receive doctorates in their early twenties.'

'Be that as it may, Dr Barclay, the building's closed until next week,' Frank said. 'I'm under orders not to let anyone in, not even visiting Swedish dignitaries. Why don't you guys come back Monday?'

'Ah,' Isaac said, wincing. 'Unfortunately Professor Bergstrom flies back to Stockholm first thing tomorrow morning, so tonight really is the only opportunity we'll get. Come on, Frank, no one will ever know. And I'll owe you big time.'

The security guard took another bite of jerky and chewed slowly before swallowing. 'Wish I could help, doc, but I need this job and, like I said, I'm under orders not to—'

Michael whipped the pistol from his pocket and stepped forward, cocking the hammer.

Frank tried to rise from his chair, but only got as far gripping the armrests before Michael put two bullets in his chest, knocking him out of his seat.

Isaac stood motionless for a second, his ears ringing as he blinked at the blood-splattered wall behind the desk.

'He was holding us up,' Michael explained, turning the smoking barrel back on Isaac.

'What if someone heard the shots?'

'Good point. We better make this quick then.'

Isaac felt himself slump like a puppet with the strings cut. Even if he made it through the night in one piece, his career was most certainly finished. 'Follow me,' he said. 'The elevator's this way.'

3

Michael exited the elevator on the twelfth floor of the Bereck & Hertz building and followed Barclay along a corridor lined with widely spaced doors. It was a struggle to keep the grin off his face, in part from being so close to getting what he wanted, but mainly because of the giddy, light-headed sensation he felt at taking another life. Not including Garcia, who regrettably still lived and breathed in this timeline, the security guard made it three in total.

After leaving Stapleton a week and a half ago, Michael had thought it sensible to lie low for a while and had travelled north into Oregon, passing Christmas in a motel on the outskirts of Ashland with only his briefcase for company. For a day or two he toyed with the idea of using one of his remaining pills to undo the killings, but then he'd seen a newspaper report stating that Ellis had been arrested and charged with Jimmy's murder, having apparently killed him in a fit of rage after discovering the strangled body of his daughter, and Michael had realised that fate had intervened once again, providing retribution against those who had wronged him, and his destiny was clearer than ever, his metamorphosis complete and his true nature at long last revealed to him.

Barclay stopped at the second to last door on the corridor, unlocked it and ushered Michael through, then pulled down the blinds before hitting the lights to reveal a large laboratory tainted by a lingering chemical aroma. There was a square table in the middle, buried under several towering stacks of paperwork that looked liable to topple over at any given moment, plus a long workbench against the back wall that held an array of stands, clamps, Bunsen burners and chemical containers. In the far corner was a sink stacked high with dirty apparatus.

'Dr Barclay, how can you even work like this?' Michael asked, appalled by the apparent disorder.

'Everything has its place,' Barclay muttered. Lowering Michael's briefcase to the floor, he stooped to open a cabinet beneath the central table.

Michael glanced to the wall on his right, which was given over to a wide blackboard where layers of competing equations and molecular diagrams had been scrawled in chalk over the smudged patchwork of their predecessors. 'What *is* all that?' he asked, turning back.

Barclay drew himself up, three brown pill bottles clutched to his chest and a grimace on his face like he'd just bitten into a lemon. 'Only the last eight months of my career, Michael. A career that's ruined thanks to what you just did downstairs. Let's get this over with, shall we?'

'How many doses is that?'

'Each bottle contains approximately one hundred pills,' Barclay said, holding them out to him.

'Only three hundred then?'

'That's all I've got. I'm giving you the Tetradyamide I prepared for the Department of Defence trials, Michael. Until I get the chance to manufacture more, that's all there is.'

Michael reached for the bottles, then realised he was still holding the gun and drew back, as with only one hand this presented him with something of a dilemma. After a moment's consideration, he instructed Barclay to find him something to carry them in. With a huff, Barclay set the bottles down on a corner of his table and retrieved a crumpled paper bag from a cupboard next to the sink.

'Only three hundred doses,' Michael repeated, staring at the blackboard again.

Barclay placed the bottles in the bag, folded the top over and held it out. 'Go on then,' he said when Michael made no attempt to move, 'take them.'

'And what happens after that?'

'*After*? Well, I guess I'll grovel to my fiancé in the hope she'll forgive me for missing the most important social event on the calendar, then grovel to the Department of Defence in the hope they'll accept a delay in delivery. As for you, Michael, you can take these pills and shove them up your ass, for all I care. So long as I never see you again after tonight, it doesn't much matter to me.'

'I think I have a better idea,' Michael said. 'Take a look in the case, why don't you?'

Barclay frowned, placed the paper bag on the floor, pushed back a mound of paper on the table and lifted the briefcase into the space he'd cleared. His eyes bulged as he opened the lid.

'How much is that?'

'Almost ten-thousand dollars.'

'But how?' Barclay asked, and then shook his head. 'Actually, on second thoughts, I don't want to know.'

'I won it at the races using the Tetradyamide you gave me before Christmas,' Michael told him anyway. 'Knowing the winner beforehand kind of takes the risk out of gambling, wouldn't you say?'

'Why are you even telling me this? I'm giving you all the Tetradyamide I have. What you do with it isn't my business.'

'Three hundred pills?' Michael sighed. 'It's a start, I'll give you that, but what happens when I run out?'

'I don't get it. What more could you possibly want from me?'

'That,' Michael said, and nodded toward the blackboard.

Barclay snorted. 'The *formula*? You must be even more whacked out than I realised. It's taken me *months* to perfect. You'll never be able to recreate it on your own.'

'I don't plan to,' Michael said, raising the gun again. 'You're going to do it for me.'

4

'This is some sort of joke, right?' Isaac asked, glancing up from the gun and into Michael's scarred face.

'Do you see me laughing? Think about it, Dr Barclay, with you producing Tetradyamide and me using it to alter the course of history, there's nothing we couldn't achieve. Working together, we could change the world. If its fame and fortune you want then this is your ticket.'

Briefly, Isaac visualised himself collecting his Nobel Prize as the upper echelons of the scientific community rose to a standing ovation. Lara would be in the front row, mouthing the words, 'I love you,' as she joined the rapturous applause.

He shook his head to dislodge the fantasy; there was no point even entertaining it. Michael Humboldt was unhinged, a lunatic and a killer. Getting into bed with him would be like climbing into a fish tank full of piranhas. But then what Michael had just said about altering the course of history bore stark resemblances to the many-worlds interpretation of quantum physics propounded by the much-maligned Hugh Everett III, whereby all possible alternate histories and futures were played out in a potentially infinite number of universes. Was Michael simply transitioning from one universe to another when he travelled through time? And, if so, might not there be others capable of the same feat? Assuming Isaac was still alive by tomorrow and had a job at Stribe Lyndhurst to return to, he decided to re-examine Michael's medical records at the first opportunity.

'So, what do you say?' Michael asked, interrupting his thoughts. 'Are you with me?'

Isaac's throat was suddenly dry. As he coughed to clear it, an electric shiver climbed his spine: the single dose of Tetradyamide he'd slipped into his mouth while retrieving the pill bottles from the cabinet beneath his workbench was beginning to kick in. While the effects might not be as profound as they were in Michael, soon Isaac's perception of the passage of time would begin to slow, giving him improved speed and reaction times and thereby opening a narrow window of opportunity in which to escape. All he now needed was to choose his moment carefully.

'There are ways to scientifically verify what you claim,' he said, angling for time. 'We could conduct tests in a controlled environment, after which I could present my findings to various medical journals—'

Michael flinched as if struck in the eye by a grain of sand. 'We've discussed this already, if you remember. I have no intention of becoming a caged bird again.'

'Then I'm afraid my answer is no.'

Michael cocked the hammer of his pistol. 'I urge you to reconsider.'

'What are you going to do, shoot me? Do that and you'll lose Tetradyamide forever.'

Michael lowered the gun for a moment as he worked through his options, then set his jaw and raised it again. 'You really want to test me on that? With all your research here, I'm sure I could find someone else to complete the job. I wonder if Dr McHayden might be interested?'

Isaac stepped forward, his vision clouded by a blanket of red. 'Don't you dare bring her into this! You speak her name again and I'll...I'll...'

'You'll what?' Michael asked, likewise stepping forward and then pressing the barrel of his gun to Isaac's nose. 'I really don't think you're in a position to be making threats here, Dr Barclay. Remember, I still have some of the Tetradyamide you gave me before Christmas in my case, and I can use it to get to Dr McHayden whenever I choose. So, the way I see it, there are two alternatives, you're either with me or against me. Which is it?'

Isaac sighed. 'Okay, you win again. You leave me no choice, I'll give you what you want.'

Michael smiled and lowered the gun. 'Goood,' he said, his voice low and slurred. 'Innn thaaat caaaase, I'll haaaave thoooose pillsss noooow.'

Moving as slowly as possible, Isaac bent to retrieve the bag of Tetradyamide from the floor. As he straightened up, Michael slowly dropped the pistol into his coat pocket and reached to take it, the action slow and lumbering.

This was it: Isaac's opportunity had come.

He swung the bag, connecting with the left side of Michael's face. The paper ripped on impact, coming apart in slow motion. Michael's fedora hat was knocked clean off his head. He doubled over, emitting a distorted shriek as a shower of pills and broken glass drifted to the floor.

Isaac darted to the workbench by the sink and snatched up a Bunsen burner. Turning back, he saw Michael jerkily stagger forward, blood streaming from multiple cuts to his face.

Isaac raised the Bunsen burner above his head and, using every ounce of his strength, brought it down on the base of the other man's skull.

5

December 1969 – January 1970

Isaac watched Michael's body crumple slowly to the floor and then turned away, the Bunsen burner slipping from his hands. He had just used Tetradyamide to kill an armed man, as successful a demonstration of the drug's potential to create more efficient soldiers as one could wish for. But short of giving Michael the formula, something that could never be allowed in the knowledge of what he was capable of, it had been his only option, especially after Michael had threatened Lara.

One of the pill bottles in the bag had shattered, but the other two remained intact. Although Tetradyamide now made it difficult to estimate how much time had elapsed since Michael had shot Frank in the foyer, the police were yet to arrive on the scene, and with any luck the sound of gunfire had been mistaken for an early firework. Still, there was much to do and it was imperative that Isaac worked fast, which, as it happened, was another of the drug's benefits.

Without further delay he fetched a new paper bag from the cupboard by the sink and set about sweeping the mixture of broken glass and loose pills into a pile, his actions a blur. When certain he hadn't missed anything, he scooped the pile into the bag, ignoring the cuts to his hands, and then dropped the unbroken bottles in too. After depositing the paper bag and Michael's briefcase by the door, he searched the chemical storage cabinet at the back of the lab, where he found several industrial-size bottles of ethanol. The whole process seemed to last several minutes, however could only have taken a fraction of that in real time.

Pulling a bottle out, he cast a final glance around the place where he'd spent so many happy, productive hours absorbed in his work. Then he unscrewed the lid and emptied the contents over the papers on his central worktable, ethanol slopping out as sluggishly as if it were treacle. When the bottle was empty, he tossed it to the floor, fetched a new one and repeated the process on the long workbench against the wall.

Standing back, he struck a match and looked on as the sulphur slowly ignited. It seemed a shame, but if his career was already finished, as he felt certain it was, he didn't want anyone picking up where he'd left off.

As the flame reached the wood, he threw the match onto the central table. It arced slowly through the air before landing in the middle of a pile of ethanol-drenched paper. At first nothing happened, but then the flames gradually spread out, expanding to a tall pillar of fire that singed his hair. Without Tetradyamide, he guessed that the whole thing would have been pretty much instantaneous.

Holding the paper bag full of Tetradyamide in one hand and Michael's briefcase in the other, he turned his back on his old life and walked out of the burning lab.

Five minutes later, Isaac climbed into his car just as the first fireworks blossomed above, signalling the start of a new decade. As a fire truck pulled up alongside him, he started the engine and then drove through the night, stopping only for gas.

6

Michael was back in the jungle, surrounded by the hum of nocturnal insect life. The dense night air hung like a fog, clogging his lungs. Perspiration ran freely down his face and neck, wetting the collar of his uniform. He glanced down to see a rifle in his hands.

Hands. Two of them. Something about this didn't seem quite right.

Suddenly he heard a sound: the unmistakable sob of a child. Though every fibre of his being screamed not to, he found himself stepping over a bank of sandbags and beginning up an overgrown path between gnarled and twisted trees that seemed to writhe with his every step. Vines and branches tugged at his clothing, pulling him back like desperate claws. He pressed on, however, compelled by some external force.

After another few yards he saw a faint movement up ahead, barely perceptible in the dark. 'Who's there?' he called out.

The sobbing stopped.

Michael took a step closer, and another. It was then that he saw her: a girl at the foot of a tree, a conical straw hat in her lap and her head buried in her arm. There was something achingly familiar yet impossible to place about her.

'I know you,' he said, lowering his rifle. 'Why?'

The girl looked up. A red-hot ember glowed in each of her eye sockets. 'I am your destiny,' she said.

As he turned to run, a spear of pain penetrated the back of his head, sending him sprawling. He took a mouthful of dirt, then rolled onto his back to see the girl standing over him. The embers in her eyes grew, flames engulfing her face and then extending over her body. They spread out from her sandaled feet and started to consume the undergrowth and trees, until eventually a circular wall of fire surrounded the pair. Michael felt his skin crackle and melt.

By now the girl's face was no more than scorched skull. She opened her jaw to speak again, billows of smoke escaping. 'Hey, man, can you hear me?'

Michael screamed and raised his hands to cover his eyes. His right hand had vanished, replaced by a metal hook on which reflected flames flickered.

The smouldering skeleton reached down, grabbed him under the shoulders and began dragging him back through the jungle. Except suddenly it wasn't forest floor beneath him anymore but bubbling lino. The blazing canopy above had become a smoke-stained ceiling. A window exploded with a loud crack, showering them with splinters of broken glass.

'Let go of me,' Michael mumbled.

'It's okay, man. I've got you. You think you can walk?'

Michael looked up. Instead of a flaming skull, he saw a man in a fire fighter's helmet staring down at him. He staggered to his feet, swaying as he was seized by a bout of coughing that felt like razor blades slicing through his lungs.

'C'mon, let's get you out of here,' the fire fighter said, placing an arm around his shoulders and helping him upright.

'Where am I?' Michael asked.

'The Bereck & Hertz building. There's a fire.'

'Bereck & Hertz?'

'You know, the pharmaceutical company. You're an employee, right?'

'Barclay,' Michael said, shrugging the man's arm from his shoulders as he remembered what had been done to him.

'What, there's someone else up here with you?'

Michael glanced about. The lab was a blazing inferno, the central table barely visible among the giant tongues of fire and thick, noxious smoke. His briefcase and the paper bag containing his bottles of Tetradyamide were nowhere to be seen. There could be only one conclusion: after trying to kill him, Barclay had robbed him blind.

'No,' he said, 'just me.'

'Okay, let's get you out of here.'

Michael nodded and allowed the fire fighter to lead him from the room. Keeping low to the ground, they followed the corridor to a stairwell at the near end. The fire fighter shoved the door open with his shoulder, bundled Michael through and let it swing shut behind them.

The air here was cleaner. Michael sucked in a grateful breath, but was immediately overwhelmed by another bout of coughing.

'Take it easy,' the fire fighter said, leaning against the handrail and raising the visor on his helmet. 'You must've breathed in a lot of smoke back there. A few more minutes and you'd have been toast, my friend.'

'Thanks.'

'Don't mention it. My truck was first on the scene, but I'm guessing the paramedics will have arrived by now, so we can get someone qualified to examine you when we get outside.'

'Paramedics?

'Sure, paramedics, fire fighters, cops, the whole emergency service gang. By the way, you're bleeding pretty heavily. I'll bet they'll want to take a look at your head to see if you've sustained a concussion. You don't remember what happened back there, do you?'

Michael reached behind his head and rubbed his fingertips over the bloody mess where Barclay had struck him. The wound hurt like hell, but however much he would have liked some proper medical attention, he'd only end up in a cell again if he followed the fire fighter from the building. Lowering his hand to his coat pocket, he was surprised to find Jimmy's pistol still residing there. Clearly fate had intervened again, and in his haste Barclay had overlooked that detail.

Michael pulled the gun out.

'Hey, whatcha doing?' the fire fighter asked, blinking at him, incredulous. 'I just saved your skin back there!'

'So you did,' Michael said, cocking the hammer, 'but I'm afraid I'm going to need your uniform and helmet too.'

The man didn't move for a second, then hurriedly stripped down to his underwear. 'I don't get it,' he said as he laid his helmet on the floor. 'Who are you?'

Michael released the hammer and returned the gun to his pocket. 'I am your destiny,' he replied, and shoved him in the chest.

The fire fighter teetered on the edge of the landing for a moment, arms cart-wheeling for purchase before gravity won out and down he went, twisting and bouncing and then hitting the landing below with a sickening crunch.

Feeling the giddy, light-headed sensation again, Michael began unbuttoning his shirt. That made it four in total.

OTHER BOOKS IN
THE PAGES OF TIME SERIES

About the Author

Damian Knight lives in London with his wife and their two daughters. He works in a library and, being surrounded by books, probably has the best day job ever. When not writing, reading, parenting or working, he often falls asleep fully clothed on the sofa.

The Pages of Time Series includes *The Pages of Time (Book 1)*, *A Trick of the Light (Book 1.5)*, *Ripples of the Past (Book 2)* and *Shadows of the Future (Book 3)*.

To find out more or get in touch, please visit www.damianknightauthor.co.uk or email damianknightauthor@gmail.com

If you enjoyed the book, reviews on Amazon and Goodreads would be very welcome.

Printed in Great Britain
by Amazon